"Go on inside and lock the doors. You never know who could be lurking around here."

"You're very good at giving me new things to worry about," Jasmine said.

Eli gave her a smile. "I'm also very good at keeping people safe."

"Sarah and I don't need you to keep us safe. We're fine on our own."

"Are you?" He leaned in close to stare into her eyes.

She wanted to move away, but she was frozen in place, fascinated by this strong, handsome man.

"Yes, we are. We've both been on our own for a while and managed just fine."

"That was then. This is now. There's real trouble here, Jasmine. If you're not careful, it will find you."

His words chilled her to the core, but she didn't want to let him know how much, or just how desperately she wished she did have someone to count on besides herself and her ailing mother-in-law. "If it does, I'll deal with it."

"And I'll be right here to help you out."

Books by Shirlee McCoy

Love Inspired Suspense

Die Before Nightfall #5
Even in the Darkness #14
When Silence Falls #18
Little Girl Lost #40
Valley of Shadows #61
Stranger in the Shadows #76
Missing Persons #88
Lakeview Protector #99

Steeple Hill Single Title

Still Waters

SHIRLEE McCOY

has always loved making up stories. As a child, she daydreamed elaborate tales in which she was the heroine—gutsy, strong and invincible. Though she soon grew out of her superhero fantasies, her love for storytelling never diminished. She knew early that she wanted to write inspirational fiction, and she began writing her first novel when she was a teenager. Still, it wasn't until her third son was born that she truly began pursuing her dream of being published. Three years later she sold her first book. Now a busy mother of four, Shirlee is a homeschool mom by day and an inspirational author by night. She and her husband and children live in Maryland and share their house with a dog and a guinea pig. You can visit her Web site at www.shirleemccoy.com.

Lakeview
PROTECTOR

Shirlee
McCoy

Steeple
Hill®

Published by Steeple Hill Books™

STEEPLE HILL BOOKS

Steeple
Hill®

ISBN-13: 978-0-373-44287-4
ISBN-10:   0-373-44287-4

LAKEVIEW PROTECTOR

www.SteepleHill.com

Printed in U.S.A.

"Though the mountains be shaken and the hills be removed, yet my unfailing love for you will not be shaken nor my covenant of peace be removed," says the LORD, who has compassion on you.

—*Isaiah* 54:10

To Aunt Jessica, who knows more than most
what it means to grieve and go on.

ONE

Frozen rain fell from steel-gray clouds, pinging off the blacktop and pattering into Smith Mountain Lake. Aside from that the day was silent, the summer bustle of guests replaced by winter solitude. Jasmine Hart was glad. People brought cash, but they also brought baggage, and she wasn't talking the kind that held clothes. Marital strife, teens with secrets, men and women hiding from the world and from their problems. She'd dealt with them all during her time at Lakeview Retreat, but that had been years ago.

Now she had her own baggage, her own secrets, her own reasons to hide, and dealing with people wasn't something she wanted to do. It seemed, though, that she had no choice in the matter. One phone call in the middle of the night, one brief conversation with her mother-in-law's best friend and Jasmine had been on a plane and flying from New Hampshire to Lakeview, Virginia. Three days later, she was caring for her mother-in-law and readying the neglected retreat for the first renter it had had in seventeen months.

Which just went to show how quickly things could change.

"Jazz! Hey, Jazz!" Karen Morris hurried across the slippery pavement, her round cheeks flushed, her brown eyes filled with youthful exuberance. A college student who worked part-time at Lakeview Retreat, Karen had enthusiasm and peppiness to spare. Jasmine tried hard not to hold that against her.

"What's up?"

"Ms. Sarah. She's awake and asking if the cabin is ready yet."

"Tell her I'll have it ready before our guest arrives. Then you'd better head home. The weather doesn't look like it's going to clear."

"Ms. Sarah said I should give you a hand cleaning the cabin." Even as she said it, Karen's gaze was darting toward the rusty Impala she'd driven to work that morning.

"She probably didn't know how bad the weather was getting."

"Maybe not, but I can't afford to get fired from this job." Karen glanced at the car again. Obviously, the thought of leaving appealed to her. Jasmine couldn't blame her. The once-bustling retreat had become a lonely place, haunted by memories and silence. Or maybe that was only Jasmine's perception of it. Maybe to others it was the same peaceful lakeside resort it had always been.

She forced her maudlin thoughts away, refocusing on Karen. "Sarah isn't going to fire you for going home when the weather is like this."

"I guess you're right. And it *is* getting slippery out here. If you need me to come this weekend, I can. It might be good to have an extra set of hands since you've got a renter now." It might be, but there wasn't money for it. At least not in Sarah's coffers. Since Jasmine's mother-in-law didn't believe in taking handouts, even from family, that was the only way the extra help could be paid for.

"I'll give you a call if I need you. Now hurry up and tell Sarah you're leaving. I don't want you out on the roads when it's this slippery." She forced a smile, waving Karen back toward the house, her stomach churning with anxiety and frustration. Things were bad. Worse than she ever could have imagined when she'd agreed to come help Sarah recover from surgery. Payback for staying away so long? Probably. And probably Jasmine deserved it.

Icy wind sliced through her thick sweatshirt and heavy parka, stealing her breath and reminding her of home. New Hampshire would have snow this week. Here in Lakeview, there'd be frozen rain, drizzle, thick clouds. The lake. Memories of Christmases and laughter. The girls dancing around the living room of Sarah's modest home. John. Solid. Dependable. All three frozen in time, suspended in her mind as they had been, not as they might have become.

Three years tomorrow.

Maybe she shouldn't keep track.

She forced the thoughts and images from her mind, refusing to dwell on the past or to contemplate the empty future. One moment at a time. One day at a time. That was the only way she'd survive.

The first of Sarah's five guest cabins was just up ahead. Small, cozy, great view of Smith Mountain Lake, it was the perfect place for solitude and peace. It wasn't what the renter had wanted though. He'd done his research online and called with a particular rental in mind. Three bedrooms, two bathrooms, set on a hill overlooking the lake, Meadow Lark cabin had always been reserved for large families. In years past, a single-occupant renter would have taken a smaller cabin or looked for a rental somewhere else. Things were different now. Sarah couldn't afford to turn business away, and Eli Jennings was welcome to Meadow Lark.

Wind buffeted the cabin, shaking windows and shutters as Jasmine stepped inside. January wasn't kind. It brought gray clouds. Cold weather. Loneliness. Death. Maybe Jazz was in the minority thinking that, but she doubted it. There had to be plenty of other people who'd just as soon skip the month.

She pulled linens from the closet, inhaled staleness and age. They'd have to be washed. She'd do the curtains in the bedroom while she was at it. No sense doing a partial job. It was an adage her mother had lived by. One she'd taught Jazz. Lately, though, doing nothing seemed preferable to doing anything at all.

Three years. Ticking by. One slow moment at a time. Drifting through her fingers like air. Gone.

And now she was back where it had all begun. Back where she'd met John, where he'd proposed, where they'd spent every vacation for thirteen years, where the girls had laughed and giggled, learned to fish, to boat, to dance in the moonlight and in the sun.

Jazz blinked back tears and shoved the linens into the small washing machine, started the water and realized too late that she didn't have detergent with her.

"Wonderful. Now I've got to go back to the house." Back to the modest rancher and its memory-filled rooms. Back to Sarah and her broken hip and strangely blank eyes. As much as the retreat had changed, Sarah had changed more, fading, shrinking, becoming a shadow of the vibrant woman she'd been.

Jazz shoved the cabin's door open with more force than necessary, stepping out onto the covered front porch and nearly walking into a tall, broad-shouldered he-man. Dark blond hair cropped short, hazel eyes surrounded by lashes any woman would be proud of, a scowl that sharpened the hard edges of his jaw and cheekbones.

Handsome.

She shoved the thought away as quickly as it came. Noticing men and what they looked like felt too much like a betrayal. "Can I help you?"

"That depends." He had a deep Southern drawl that was much warmer than his expression.

"On?"

"On whether or not you're Jasmine Hart."

"That depends." She leaned back against the door.

His scowl deepened. "On?"

"On who wants to know."

A tiny smile flicked across his hard features before it disappeared. "Eli Jennings. I've got reservations."

"Nice to meet you, Mr. Jennings. I'm glad you made it here with the weather being so bad, but, as I told you last night, check-in is at three."

"I was hoping you wouldn't mind letting me check in early. Mrs. Hart down at the main house didn't seem to think you would."

"Sarah would be right on most occasions, but the cabin hasn't been used in a while. It needs to be aired out and cleaned. I'll need time to do it."

"I'll take care of it." The finality in his tone refused any further argument, and Jasmine shrugged.

"You're welcome to move your stuff in now, then."

"Glad to hear it." There went the tiny smile again, a subtle tilting of his lips that softened his hard features, but didn't ease the coldness in his eyes.

He'd said he was a writer when he'd called the night before, but his broad, muscled frame and taut expression belonged on a military man, a cop. A career criminal. Whatever he was, whoever he was, that was his business. As long as he paid the rent on time, she'd leave Eli Jennings and his secrets alone. "I've started the linens and curtains. I'm just running down to the house to get detergent."

"I've got everything I need in my truck."

Jazz pushed away from the door. "Here's the key then.

You've got a phone line. Dial-up Internet access. Television with cable. Nothing fancy."

"If I wanted fancy I'd be at the Hilton." His smile took the sting out of the words and stole the breath from Jasmine's lungs. Not a tiny smile this time. A full-blown, melt-a-woman's-heart smile. No man should have a smile that warm, that decadent.

She blinked, took a step away. It was definitely time to leave.

She strode toward the porch steps, forgetting the icy rain until her foot slipped and she fell backward.

Hard hands wrapped around her waist, jerking her upright, reminding her of what a man's touch was like—strong, steady, sure.

"Better watch your step, ma'am. The ice is making things treacherous."

Ma'am? She was thirty-three. Not ninety. And unless she missed her guess, Jennings was a few years older. "Jazz is fine. Or Jasmine."

His cold hazel eyes raked her from the tip of her scuffed boots to the top of the knit cap she wore. "Jasmine."

Warm honey. Sweet tea. Deep South manners wrapped in six foot two of attitude and trouble.

Jazz looked away, disconcerted, guilty and angry at herself for being both. "If you need anything, call the house. The number's near the phone."

"Will do."

"If you decide to extend your stay another month, rent is due on the first. You leave before the month is up, there's no refund."

"So you told me last night."

"Just making sure we're clear, Mr. Jennings."

"Eli. And we're very clear." He smiled again, the fine lines near his eyes deepening, his muted hazel gaze now forest-green.

Definitely handsome.

Definitely trouble.

Definitely someone Jazz should stay far away from.

She took her time retreating down the stairs, absolutely sure she didn't want Eli's hands on her waist again. It was bad enough that she could sense his steady gaze following her as she maneuvered the slippery path that led to the gravel drive. She didn't need to feel the warmth of his fingers pressing into her sides.

A large SUV was parked on the driveway, and Jazz bypassed it, noticing the details even as she told herself they weren't important. Black tinted windows made it impossible to see inside. Was he hiding something in there? A pet? A person? Something else? If he hadn't been watching, she'd have given in to curiosity and peeked in the front window.

She sidled around the car, her feet slipping out from under her again. She slid forward, banging into the door of the SUV and grabbing on to the hood to steady herself.

"Seems like you're having a little trouble with the ice. Maybe I should give you a ride back to your house." Eli spoke close to her ear, his voice so unexpected, Jazz's heart leaped to her throat.

She straightened, forcing herself to meet his gaze, and ignoring the quick flutter of her stomach as she did so. "Thanks for the offer, but I can manage."

"Suit yourself." He moved past, popped open the back door of the SUV and pulled out two brown paper bags. A box of Froot Loops peeked out of the top of one. It was almost enough to distract Jazz from the rifle case lying across the backseat.

Almost.

She didn't like firearms of any kind, and was pretty sure she didn't like the idea of her new renter having one in the cabin. "Planning to do some hunting?"

He followed the direction of her gaze, and flashed straight white teeth. "My dad is the hunter in the family. I've got camera equipment in there."

"Strange place to store camera equipment."

"You should see where I keep the rifle."

"Should I ask?"

"Not unless you really want to know." He threw another smile in her direction and started back up to the house, leaving Jazz to wonder if he was serious or kidding.

That was the trouble with keeping people at a distance. You stopped picking up subtle clues about their thoughts and feelings, about their truthfulness or lack thereof. That wasn't a problem when you chose to hide away from life. It became one when you stepped back out into the world.

Or when you were yanked kicking and screaming back into it. Which was pretty much how Jazz's reemergence had happened.

She shook her head, trudging back toward the rancher. Sarah would be waiting for breakfast, probably sitting in the kitchen, her too-thin fingers wrapped around a book, her soft-eyed gaze eating up the fairy-tale story written on its pages. No doubt she'd glance up when Jazz walked in, smile that easy smile of hers that was so much like John's, ask what Jazz thought of their new renter.

Act as if no more than time had passed between Jazz and herself even though they both knew that the truth was much darker and uglier than that. Three years since Jazz had last set foot on Lakeview Retreat land. She'd grieved during that time. Alone. Concerned only for herself. While Sarah had struggled on her own.

Guilt had a taste. It was bitter and hot. Jazz swallowed it down as she stepped into Sarah's house.

TWO

Like everything in Jazz's life, the rancher seemed to have faded since she'd lost her husband and daughters. She couldn't decide if her pain-shadowed perception was to blame or if the once-cheerful living room really had grown dim and dreary. Bright blues and crisp whites seemed muted and dingy, the once-pristine area now cluttered with magazines and books.

Jazz picked up a few as she stepped through the room, sliding them back into place on the bookshelves that lined one wall, barely glancing at titles or photographs. She knew what they were. Celebrity rags, romance novels, nothing academic. None of the autobiographies or biographies Sarah had once loved reading. Jazz couldn't blame her mother-in-law for burying herself in romanticized tales. If she could have, she would have done the same. But for Jazz there was no comfort in fantasy and fairy tale, only the grim reality of life lived without those she loved.

"Is that you, Jasmine?" Sarah called out, a hint of anxiety coloring her words. Jazz wanted to ignore it, but ignoring the paranoia that her mother-in-law seemed to suffer from was nearly impossible. Over the past three days, Jazz had waged constant battle against Sarah's fears.

"Who else would it be?" She hurried into the kitchen, a smile firmly in place.

"You never know, dear. You just never know." Sarah's answering smile was exactly as Jazz had known it would be—John, Maddie, Megan, all rolled into one, squeezing Jazz's lungs and stealing her breath.

"Well, this time, you do. It's me. Back to make you breakfast."

"Coffee will be fine."

"You need more than that, Sarah. How about some eggs? Bacon? Pan-fried potatoes?"

"Coffee." Sarah's tone brooked no argument, her fingers tapping against the paperback book that sat in front of her on the table, her shoulders hunched and bowed. Too thin, too frail.

This time it was Jazz's heart that clenched. "You have to eat, Sarah."

"Do I?" Sarah smiled again, but the look in her eyes was flat and dead, as if modern medicine had trapped a soul that should have already departed.

Jazz reached for her hand, squeezing. "You can't heal if you don't eat. How about just a piece of toast?"

It looked as if Sarah would refuse, the tilt to her chin, the tightness of her pale lips reminding Jazz of other times—John and Sarah equally matched in stubborn determination and standing on opposite sides of an issue, staring each other down, neither willing to concede. In the end they'd always come together again, laughing about their stubbornness, teasing each other in the timeless mother-son dance of affection.

Without John as a foil, it seemed Sarah's stubbornness had faded. She shrugged. "Toast then."

"And a banana?"

"Don't push your luck, dear." The response was more Sarah-like than any other in the few days Jazz had been there. She hoped it was a good sign.

"Toast. Coffee. And later I'm going out for a dozen of Doris's éclairs."

"In this weather? Do you really think that's a good idea?"

"I'm used to this kind of weather. Besides, I've been craving éclairs since I got here."

"You're hoping to tempt more calories into me, is more likely the case."

"That's true, too."

"Then feel free to bring a dozen éclairs home. I may just have it in me to eat one. While you're at it, maybe you could stop by Kitty's Little Book Shoppe. I'm almost out of reading material."

"I can definitely do that. Or we can go together tomorrow." Jazz set coffee and toast on the table in front of her mother-in-law, then took the chair across from her. "After the doctor's appointment you've got in the morning."

"Don't remind me about the appointment. More poking and prodding. It would have been better if the person trying to murder me had been successful. No doubt, he's enjoying my slow torture."

"Don't talk like that, Sarah. Of course it wouldn't have been better if you'd died." Jazz shifted in her seat, wishing she could turn the conversation to a safer subject. Sarah claimed she'd been shoved down a flight of stairs during the grand opening of a Civil War museum housed in a restored mansion. The local sheriff disagreed. He had witnesses who had seen Sarah's fall. Jasmine was inclined to believe his version, the fact that she doubted her mother-in-law's account proving just how much their relationship had changed.

She covered Sarah's hand with her own, trying to convey

a calm she didn't feel. "You seem down, Sarah. Maybe I should call the doctor. Have him come over and make sure you're okay."

"*Down* as in loony and paranoid, right?" Sarah scowled, her eyes flashing, slashes of pink coloring her pale cheeks.

"No. *Down* as in depressed. The doctor said trauma can cause that sometimes."

"Well, not in me. I'm about as far from depressed as a person can get. What I am is angry. Angry that the sheriff doesn't believe I'm in danger and angry that you don't. Angry that everyone would rather believe I'm paranoid than believe the truth."

"Sarah—"

"Don't, Jasmine. I know what the doctors have told you. They think I'm losing it. They'll be proven wrong eventually. Of course, by that time it might be too late." Sarah lifted her book, pretending to turn her attention back to the story, but Jasmine could tell from her frown that the conversation wasn't over.

"I know you're frustrated, but a half a dozen people saw you fall down those stairs. No one saw you being pushed." The words slipped out before Jazz thought them through, and she regretted them immediately.

"There were hundreds of people at the grand opening of the museum. No one was watching one old lady walking down the stairs, so how could anyone know for sure what happened? Anyone but me, that is." Sarah's gaze speared into Jazz's, flecks of gold and green standing out against the dark blue. John's eyes looking into Jazz's, accusing, pleading.

She lowered her gaze, fiddling with a napkin, searching for just the right words, but knowing she wouldn't find them. Words used to come easily. Not anymore. She struggled and searched and still came up wanting. "I believe you."

Simple. Direct. Not quite the truth.

Wanting to believe didn't mean a person actually *did* believe.

She'd learned that the hard way over the past years as she'd fought to hold onto what little faith she'd had.

"No. You don't, but it's all right. I love you anyway. I'm going to rest for a while. Tell me before you go out, okay?"

"Okay."

The house fell silent as Sarah shuffled away, leaning on her walker—bent, older than her years, faded in some indefinable way.

That was what grief did—it aged the body, stole from the mind, made every hour into a hundred, every day into an eternity.

Jasmine grabbed the empty toast plate and the still-full coffee mug from the table, forcing somber thoughts away. She'd come here to help. Her sadness could only make things worse, her doubts feeding rather than assuaging Sarah's paranoia.

If it *was* paranoia.

The doctors seemed to think so. Jazz was…undecided. Exactly the way she was about everything in her life.

She lifted Sarah's book from the table, the cover's pastel colors highlighting a man, a woman and a little girl who danced between them. Jazz's life had been like that once— sunlight and shadows, laughter and tears, balanced out by love, affection, companionship.

Now it was different.

Not bad.

Not particularly good.

Just different.

Many of her friends thought she should get back into the dating game, start seeing people. Others suggested she adopt, bring children into her home, let laughter chase away the sorrow.

Jazz knew she could do both, but she couldn't replace what was lost and had no desire to try. Instead, she lived life on her own terms, ignoring her friends' suggestions. Even though that meant facing her life alone.

The business line rang, and she grabbed it, thankful for the distraction. "Lakeview Retreat, can I help you?"

"May I speak to Mrs. Jasmine Hart?"

"This is she."

"My name is Keith Sherman. I've heard that your mother-in-law is having some financial difficulties."

"Heard from whom?"

"Friend of a friend. I'm a real-estate investor, and I'd be very interested in purchasing her property. I'm sure you can see what a good idea that would be. Medical expenses for the elderly can be quite high."

"Sarah isn't elderly, and she's not interested in selling."

"Whether she's interested in it or not isn't the point. She's probably got an emotional attachment to the place, but I'm sure you could help her see past that."

"I'm not going to talk her into something she doesn't want, if that's what you're hinting at."

"So, you'd rather see her lose the property to the bank?"

"She's not going to lose the property to the bank."

"That's not what I'm hearing."

"It is now. Thanks for your query, Mr. Sherman." She hung up before he could say more, her heart hammering a quick, hard beat.

Lose the property to the bank?

Were things really that bad?

Jazz had looked through the past year's books when she'd arrived, had realized how little revenue had come in, but she hadn't bothered opening the mail piled up on Sarah's desk, or checking her mother-in-law's bank statements. Sarah was a private person. She didn't believe in sharing burdens or responsibilities, and would never allow others to look into her finances. She had a strict code of ethics. Honesty, hard work, repaying debts; those were principles Sarah lived by. Jasmine couldn't believe that had changed.

She hurried into the office, sat down at the desk, grabbing the pile of mail and sorting through it. Bills were piled to her left, correspondences to the right, junk mail in the trash can. It took three hours, but she finally finished, her heart sinking as she reread the letter threatening foreclosure.

The caller had been right. Sarah was about to lose her property. Jazz reached for the phone, hesitated, knowing her mother-in-law wouldn't be happy with what she was about to do. If John were alive, he'd have prayed, approached his mother with a plan of action, then followed through in whatever way he felt led while Jazz watched in awe, wishing her own prayers could be answered as quickly and decisively. She'd thought that once she matured as a Christian they would be, that she'd hear God's voice more clearly, understand more easily the direction she was supposed to take.

Somehow, though, spiritual growth had never happened. While John's faith had flourished, hers had stayed in infancy. Even as she'd prayed with Megan and Maddie, rejoiced as they'd taken their own fledgling steps of faith, she'd wondered and doubted and worried and questioned and asked herself if what lived in her soul was less real than what lived in John's and her daughters'.

At the time of their deaths, she still hadn't found an answer. Now, she didn't care to try. Being part of their faith experience wasn't necessary anymore. What *was* necessary was action. She'd let Sarah down too many times in the past few years. That was obvious. Whether her mother-in-law would thank her or not, Jazz intended to make up for that in the only way she could. She lifted the phone and dialed the number of the bank.

THREE

Nighttime was the worst for Jasmine. The empty space beside her in bed. The silence. The hollowness of the house. The best thing, Jazz found, was to keep busy until she couldn't keep her eyes open any longer, then fall into a restless, dream-filled sleep. Often John and the girls would be waiting for her there, their laughter following her from dreams into daylight. That was when she understood how deep and true love was, how impossible it was to measure or to confine. It reached beyond time, beyond death, filling the heart even when arms were empty.

Tonight, with Sarah settled into her room and the tap of icy rain hitting windows and roof, Jazz still felt the aloneness of the night, the emptiness that yawned beside her in bed. At a little after midnight, she was still awake, sketching illustrations for an alphabet book. A tiger. Friendly-looking to go with the cute little rhyme that would be on the page. The only problem was Jazz's tiger looked more ferocious than friendly, his snarling face and jagged stripes enough to scare even the bravest toddler away.

"Focus, Jazz. This thing is due in ten days." She muttered the words as she ripped the drawing from the pad, tossed it into the trash can and tapped her pencil against the bed. This should be easy, so why was she struggling with it?

Maybe because being bombarded with photos of John and the girls that sat on every table and shelf in Sarah's house had stolen her ability to concentrate. Maybe because she was still worried about the financial help she'd given Sarah and what Sarah's response to that would be. Maybe because she was still thinking about the guest in Meadow Lark cabin—his rifle case, his warm smile, his hard eyes.

Maybe all of the above.

And maybe she should just forget all those things and finish the tiger, the umbrella bird, the vixen, the walrus, the yak and the zebra so she could mail the assignment out.

She smoothed a hand over a clean page, glancing at the storyboard she'd been sent. An easy assignment. Get it done. Get it out the door. Decide if this was really what she wanted to spend the rest of her life doing—drawing pictures for someone else's stories while her Danielle Donkey stories were reprinted over and over again. That was all she needed to do. Simple.

A line. Two. Curves. Shapes, coming together to form the sketch. She'd just finished the tiger's smiling mouth when a scream rent the air, high pitched and terror filled, heartrending in its fevered intensity.

"Sarah!" Jazz ran across the room, the sketch pad falling from icy fingers, her heart tripping in her chest as she raced for her mother-in-law's room, shoved the door open.

The light was off and she flicked it on, inhaling the musty scent of age and medicine, and the coppery scent of fear. Her mother-in-law pressed up against the headboard of her bed, her eyes wide and feverishly bright against pale skin, her gaze fixed on the window.

"Sarah? What's wrong? Are you okay?"

"It's out there, watching me." The hoarse whisper was almost as terrifying as Sarah's scream.

"What? What's out there?" Jazz moved toward the window, fear quivering in her throat and belly, images flashing through her head. Bogeymen, ghosts, other things that didn't exist except in the imagination.

"The thing that's trying to kill me."

"There's nothing there." Was there? Jazz pressed her face against the glass, peering into the darkness and trying to see shapes in the shadows.

"Call the police. Call them now before he gets in."

"You saw a *man* outside the window?" That made more sense, though the idea of a man lurking outside seemed almost as unbelievable as a phantom creature. Even a serial killer would hesitate to be out on a night like this.

"I saw something. A shadow with milk-white eyes."

"Sarah…"

"Someone was out there. Call the police before he gets away." She sounded more rational now, more believable, and Jasmine grabbed the phone from the bedside table, dialing the sheriff's department rather than 911. No sense tying up the emergency line for something that probably wasn't an emergency. Maybe her mother-in-law had had a nightmare, or maybe she'd really seen something. One way or another, Jazz was pretty sure they were safe inside the house.

Sirens drew Eli Jennings to the living-room window of his rental, their screaming frenzy carrying over the sound of the winter storm. Outside, ice still fell, collecting on the grass and trees and sparkling in the light that spilled out from the window. Down the hill and to the left, blue and white lights flashed. Unless he missed his guess, they were near the small rancher he'd visited earlier. Not that it was any of his business. Then again, he'd never cared too much about whether things were his business. That was why he was in Lakeview, Virginia, instead of at home in Atlanta. And that was why he was about to take a midnight walk in icy rain.

He grabbed his jacket from the coat closet and stepped out the front door. Probably this was a bad idea. Probably he shouldn't be doing it. But two women lived down in that rancher, one too frail to protect herself, one so brittle Eli thought a strong wind might shatter her.

Not his business, sure, but Eli was hardwired to protect. The weak, the fragile, the frail. Those who couldn't fight for themselves. It was why he'd joined the military and why he'd still be in it if he could. Unfortunately, the choice had been taken out of his hands. A roadside bomb and suddenly he was Stateside, near deaf in one ear, and sporting a roadmap of scars and a pronounced limp. Seeing as how five of his buddies hadn't survived the attack, Eli figured he had more to be thankful for than to complain about.

He made his way down the steep slope that led away from the cabin, moving past his SUV and along the gravel driveway that led to the Harts' house. He'd done his research before he'd arrived, knew exactly who his landlords were. At least who they were on paper. Jasmine Hart—well-known children's book author and illustrator, faded to obscurity after the death of her husband and daughters, living a quiet life in New Hampshire until her mother-in-law fell down a flight of stairs and fractured her skull and her hip. Sarah Hart—owner of Lakeview Retreat. Widowed young. Raised a son. On the verge of losing the property she'd worked so hard for.

Those were the facts.

Reality was different. Reality was the frail, older woman who'd shuffled along with a walker while offering him tea, and the younger woman who'd looked like more trouble than Eli had time for. From the tip of her multicolored knit cap to the soles of her scuffed brown boots, she had the kind of can't-hurt-me attitude that could put a person into all kinds of dangerous situations. Tough. Strong. A survivor. But brittle, too. Like overstressed glass, she might shatter at any moment.

He'd met other women like her. In Africa, Afghanistan and Iraq. Different places. Same stories. Military life had put him in contact with plenty of people whose lives had unfolded in horrifying tableaux. Jazz was no different.

Except for her eyes.

Not blue. Not green. A mixture of colors that reminded him of Asia's deep valleys and lush jungles, of hazy mornings and strong, dark coffee. The fact that he'd noticed just proved how much trouble she was going to be. He had a job to do, and that job didn't include comparing a woman's eyes to foliage.

Two police cars were parked in front of Sarah's house, and he skirted around them, stopping when a harsh voice called from the open doorway of the rancher. "You looking for someone, friend?"

"Just making sure everything is all right." He waited until the officer moved into sight. "I'm Eli Jennings. One of the Harts' renters."

"Must be a pretty new one. As far as I know, none of the cabins have been rented in over a year."

"I just drove in today."

"Staying long?"

"At least a month."

"For?"

"Business."

"What kind of business?"

"Not the kind that's going to cause you any trouble, Officer."

"Sheriff. Jake Reed." The man offered a hand, but his scowl said he wasn't happy with Eli's response. Too bad. It was all he was getting. Until Eli got a better sense of which Lakeview residents were important to his investigation, he planned to keep his purpose for being there close to the cuff. If the sheriff questioned him privately, he'd tell all. Otherwise, he had nothing more to say about his "business."

He plastered a good-old-boy smile onto his face and leaned a shoulder against a porch post. "Good to meet you, Sheriff. So, *is* everything okay?"

"Everything is fine, Mr. Jennings. Sorry for the disturbance." Jasmine emerged from the house, drowning in gray flannel pajamas, her hair a halo of wild curls around a sharp-angled face, her eyes huge pools of uncertainty.

Fine?

Eli doubted it. "It seems that if everything were okay you wouldn't have two police cars sitting in front of your house."

"Sarah thought she saw someone outside her window. I'm sure—"

"That she's a crazy old fool who's too muddled in the head to know what she's looking at." Sarah Hart appeared in the doorway, leaning heavily on her walker, her lined face pale, her knuckles white with tension.

"You know that isn't what I think." To her credit, Jasmine sounded hurt at her mother-in-law's accusation, though Eli wondered if she actually did believe Sarah's thinking was muddled.

"I *know* what I saw and what I saw was a face staring in the window at me." Sarah sagged a little as she spoke, grimacing and in obvious pain.

Jazz put a hand on her shoulder. "You need to sit down, Sarah. Jake will handle things out here. Give me a few minutes and I'll come in and make you a cup of tea."

The older woman's shoulders stiffened and her chin went up. She reminded Eli of a younger version of his grandma Fern. Soft as warm butter until someone got her back up, then she was hard as steel.

"I can handle making tea myself, and I'll handle this investigation myself, too, if no one is willing to take me seriously." She shot the sheriff a hard look that was only slightly less effective because of her frailty.

Eli turned his attention to Jake, watching for his reaction. The way he saw it, a man could be measured by the way he treated a lady. In his estimation, anyone who didn't treat a lady right didn't deserve to be called a man.

Apparently, the sheriff had the same philosophy. Despite Sarah's obvious anger, Jake's response was gentle, his words calm. "I'm taking you very seriously. If someone was here, we'll find out who and why."

"If?"

"Sarah, I've known you enough years to know that you'd rather hear the truth than a pretty lie, so I'm going to tell you what I think. I think you saw something. Whether or not that something was a person still has to be determined."

Good answer, Reed. Not too coddling, not too gruff. The truth. Plain and simple. Eli's opinion of the sheriff rose, and he pushed away from the porch pillar, ignoring Jasmine's quelling look, the sheriff's scrutiny, and the voice inside telling him to mind his own business. "Did you see a face, Mrs. Hart? Hair color? Eyes?"

"I've already taken her statement, Jennings. There's no need to go over it all again."

"Just wondering why she thought it was a person."

"I saw eyes. White eyes." Sarah shuddered, and Jasmine put a hand on her arm, aiming a dark look in Eli's direction.

"Let's go have that tea, Sarah. Would you like to join us, Sheriff?"

"Thanks, but I'm going to join my men, look around some more, then be on my way. If we find anything, I'll stop back in."

"Thank you."

"If you see anything else that has you worried, give me a call. Doesn't matter how trivial it seems."

"We will."

The sheriff nodded, then headed out into the rain, rounding the side of the house and disappearing from view.

"I guess you'll be heading back to the cabin now." It wasn't a question. As a matter of fact, Eli was fairly confident it was a request.

"Am I?" He purposely drawled the words. "And here I was hoping to join you two for a cup of tea." His mother would smack him upside the head if she knew he'd just begged an invitation, but something was going on here, and he wanted to know what.

"Since when do men drink tea?"

"We'd love to have you."

Jasmine and Sarah spoke simultaneously, and Eli answered both. "Thanks for the invitation, Mrs. Hart. I've spent a lot of time overseas and picked up the habit there."

"Overseas? Are you military, Mr. Jennings?" Sarah shuffled back into the house as she spoke and Eli followed, passing by Jasmine, who hovered near the open door. She looked confused, her blue-green eyes wide with anxiety as if she wasn't quite sure how he'd ended up in the house and wasn't exactly sure what she wanted to do about it.

"I was military. A marine. I'm retired now."

"My husband was a marine. Went to Vietnam and never came home." Tears pooled in Sarah's eyes, and Eli wished he'd left the two women alone. He'd wanted to find out what was going on, not dredge up Sarah's painful past and bring her to tears.

Which, by the way, he wasn't very good at dealing with. Sure he had four sisters, but they were more likely to cry on each other's shoulders than his.

He cleared his throat, put a hand on Sarah's thin shoulder, wondering why it was taking Jasmine so long to follow them into the kitchen. "That must have been painful for you, Mrs. Hart."

"Call me Sarah. And it *was* painful. It was also a long time ago. I shouldn't be getting teary eyed about it anymore. Chalk it up to fatigue and pain." She offered a watery smile, and Eli smiled back, thinking again that Sarah was a lot like his gran. Tough and soft all at the same time.

"I imagine that's to be expected after hip surgery."

"Hip surgery? How do you know she's had hip surgery?"

He turned to face Jasmine, surprised at the quick leap in his pulse when he met her gaze. She wasn't pretty in the conventional sense of the word, but there was something about her that commanded attention. Commanded *his* attention, anyway. The strong line of her jaw, the wide blue-green of her eyes, the dark arched brows and full lips made him want to look again and again. "My grandmother had hip surgery two years ago. She used a walker for a while. I just assumed that might be the case."

"Did you?" Jasmine's eyes bored into his, her suspicion obvious. Good instincts, but he wasn't going to admit the truth. Telling her he'd paid a fair amount of money to find out everything he could about the Hart women wasn't on Eli's agenda for the night.

"Did your grandmother have an easy recovery?" Sarah's question saved Eli from doing some verbal backpedaling, and he smiled in her direction.

"She sure did. Gran was riding horses six months later. Seeing as how she's probably a decade older than you, I'd say you'll be back to your normal activities in no time."

"I'll be back to my normal activities if I survive long enough."

Survive long enough? Now they were heading in the direction Eli wanted to go. "Is there some reason why you wouldn't?"

"Someone is trying to kill me."

"Why would someone want to do that?"

"If I knew maybe I'd be able to figure out who it was. As it is, I can't get anyone to take me seriously."

"The sheriff seemed to be taking you seriously."

"Do you think so?"

"I'm going to start the tea," Jasmine interrupted, grabbing a teapot from the stove and making a loud production of filling it with water, her tight, short movements the equivalent of a three-minute lecture titled: You Shouldn't Be Having this Conversation with My Mother-in-law.

Too bad he didn't agree. A woman had gone missing two months ago. Probably it had nothing to do with Sarah Hart's belief that someone was trying to kill her.

Probably.

On the off chance it did, Eli figured conversation on the subject wasn't out of line. "Has someone threatened you, Sarah?"

"Threatened? Pushed me down the stairs, that's what someone did. Broke my hip, gave me a concussion. It's only by the grace of God I'm still alive."

"Grace of God? If He was really gracious, He would have kept you from falling." Jasmine pulled teacups from a cupboard, her shoulders stiff, the bitter words surprising Eli. According to the report he'd received, Jasmine attended church every Sunday, gave copious amounts of money to charity, illustrated children's books for a Christian publishing company.

"I didn't *fall*. I was pushed."

The conversation had a well-worn feel to it, and Eli suspected the subject had been hashed out more than a few times. Might as well stick his nose into it and see where that took him. "Pushed by the same person who was at your window?"

"Probably."

"No."

Once again, the women spoke in tandem. This time, Eli focused his attention on Jasmine as she poured steaming water over tea bags. "It *is* possible, you know."

She raised her gaze from the tea, her feelings hidden in the blue-green depth of her eyes. "Of course it's possible, but is it likely? Ice is spitting from the sky, the ground is slick, only a fool would come out on a night like this. A fool couldn't push a woman down the stairs with dozens of people around and not be seen."

"A fool couldn't, but someone very, very smart and very, very determined might be able to."

Her eyes widened at his words, tea sloshing over the rim of the cup as her hand jerked. "That's not very comforting."

"Comforting is hot chocolate on a cold day. It'll warm you, but it won't keep you safe."

"What will?" She sized him up, her eyes moving from his head to his feet and back again. "A big strong hero?"

"I'm flattered." He grinned, not at all bothered by her sarcastic tone and more than willing to volunteer his services. "But I was thinking more along the lines of knowledge. And a good security system."

"A security system. That *is* a good idea. We should call

someone tomorrow, Jasmine. See about putting one in." Sarah lowered herself into a chair, took the tea Jasmine had set on the table.

"Sure. We can do that." Jasmine passed a cup of tea to Eli, her fingers brushing against his as he took it from her. A zing of warmth ran up his arm, lodged somewhere in the vicinity of his chest and made his heart race.

What was it about this woman?

Her eyes?

Her lips?

The toughness that barely hid her vulnerability and sadness?

Yeah. That was probably it. Eli was a sucker for the downtrodden. This time, though, he was going to have to keep his distance. He'd come to Lakeview to do a job. Getting distracted was a surefire way to be certain it didn't get done. He'd gotten the information he'd come in the house for, found out what had happened, made a practical suggestion for keeping the women safe. It was time to go.

He took a few sips of weak tea, then rinsed his cup and set it in the sink. "I'd better be on my way so you ladies can get some rest. Thanks for the tea."

"Anytime." Sarah smiled and started to rise, but he put a hand on her shoulder to keep her in place.

"No need to get up, Sarah. I can see myself out." With that, he strode from the room, determined to get back to planning his strategy for finding Rebecca McKenna. Grown women didn't just up and disappear. Not unless they were running from something. Or someone.

According to Eli's friend and former commander, Marcus Trenton, Rebecca wasn't the kind of person who'd have enemies or reasons to hide. Maybe he was right, or maybe Marcus just wanted to believe his sister innocent of what her husband had accused her—falling in love and running off with another man. One way or another, Eli was going to find out what had happened to Rebecca. He owed Marcus a lot. Even if he hadn't, he wouldn't have turned his back on a friend.

Cold wind blew across the lake, slapping icy rain into Eli's face as he made his way to the cabin. He'd come to Lakeview to find Rebecca. That was where his focus needed to be. But even as he told himself that, his mind was at the Harts' house, his brain replaying the conversation he'd had with Jasmine and Sarah. Something was going on there. Not just something. Trouble. Whether it was part of the plan or not, Eli had a feeling he was going to be seeing a lot more of the Hart women.

FOUR

"*A fool couldn't push a woman down the stairs with dozens of people around and not be seen.*"

"*A fool couldn't, but someone very, very smart and very, very determined might be able to.*"

The words ran through Jasmine's mind again and again as she poured Sarah another cup of tea, unloaded the dishwasher and placed her mug and Eli's into it.

Eli had been right, and she wasn't happy about it. Imagining someone staring in the window was bad enough. Imagining that that person was an evil mastermind determined to harm Sarah made her want to put bars on the windows and doors.

"He rinsed his cup." Sarah's words drew Jasmine from her thoughts, and she turned to face her mother-in-law.

"What?"

"Eli rinsed his cup."

"Should we give him a medal?"

"How many men do you know who clean up after themselves?"

"About the same number whose cleaning habits I know. None."

"My husband didn't clean up after himself. I remember

spending the first three months of our marriage trying to get him to pick up his socks. I bet you had the same problem with John. I know he wasn't neat when he was living at home."

At the mention of John, Jasmine's throat tightened. This was why she'd avoided Sarah for so long. Shared memories demanded voice and discussion, but only made the hurt that much harder to bear. "You're right. He wasn't neat after we married, either."

"See? That's my point. A neat man is something a woman doesn't find very often."

"So?"

"So Eli is handsome, strong, charming, neat. That's a powerful combination."

"What are you getting at, Sarah?"

"You're young, Jasmine. Maybe it's time—"

"It's not." She cut Sarah off, not wanting to get into a discussion about John, Eli, time passing. She knew it was passing. She felt it slipping away every moment of every day. That didn't mean she was ready to jump into another relationship.

"I'm sorry, dear. I didn't mean to upset you."

"You didn't. I just think we have more important things to discuss."

"Like faces in the window? Security systems? Doctor's appointments? I'd much rather spend the time before I go back to my room talking about more pleasant things. Things that aren't going to keep me awake in bed." Sarah sipped her tea and fingered the paperback book that still sat on the kitchen table, her skin parchment thin and lined with age, worry and sorrow.

Jazz's heart clenched, her stomach churning with anxiety. The last thing she wanted was to give Sarah more to worry about. "It's my turn to apologize. I wasn't thinking about how scared you must be. How about we bunk together? I can sleep on the love seat in your room."

"I couldn't ask you to do that, Jazz."

"Then it's good you don't have to." She wiped down the counter and hung the dishrag to dry. "I'll go get my pillow and a blanket. Then we'd both better get to sleep. We've got to be up and out early."

Sarah agreed, standing with difficulty and heading toward her room, the click and shuffle of her retreat fading, then stopping altogether. Jazz took her time rinsing Sarah's cup, loading it into the dishwasher. She didn't mind sharing a room, but she didn't want to talk anymore. Not about what had happened tonight and not about the past. Certainly not about men and dating. She was past those things. Way past them. She might only be thirty-three, but she felt older. Ancient even.

She sighed, grabbed her pillow and a blanket from her room and quietly entered Sarah's. The deep, even sound of her mother-in-law's breathing was a relief. No need to say good-night, no need to make conversation. Maybe she'd fall asleep just as quickly as Sarah had.

Or maybe she'd lie there until dawn listening to the house settling, staring into the dark room, wishing she could go back in time, relive all the moments that were still such a vivid part of her memories.

She blinked back unwanted tears, and moved to the window, pulling back the curtains. Night was already fading, the sky gray-blue and streaked violet with the first fingers of dawn. The rain had stopped, the silence beyond the window broken only by the soft tap of water dripping from the eaves. If she listened hard enough, Jazz imagined she could hear her daughters' laughter drifting on the morning air, caught between here and there, the time before and the time after. Not quite audible, but not silent either.

Memories. That was what other people would say. To

Jazz, the phantom sounds were imprints of lives lived with joy and vigor. Sometimes she thought if she tried hard enough, she could reach out and touch the images that had been hardwired into her brain from the moment her daughters had been born. She'd had so many hopes and dreams for them, so many memories she'd still wanted to make.

By the time dawn tinged the world with silvery-gray light, Jazz was stiff from lack of sleep, her body squeezed onto the love seat, her legs curved close to her chest. The room was lighter now, the cluttered dresser with its million and one photos of John and the girls seeming to mock Jazz's efforts to sleep. Finally, she stood, folded the blanket and left the room, determined to put the long sleepless night behind her.

She brewed a pot of coffee, left it warming as she got dressed, pulled on a coat and stepped outside. A short walk. A little time away from the house. A few minutes to regroup. She'd feel better then. Later, she'd take Sarah out to breakfast, try to get both of their minds off what had happened the night before. They'd go to Becky's Diner, have omelets and hot chocolate before they went to Sarah's doctor's appointment. It was a plan anyway, and that was a lot better than sitting around moping about what might have been but wasn't.

Ice crunched under her feet as she walked down to the lake and stepped onto the rickety dock. Wood boards wiggled as she walked, and she frowned. She'd have to call around, see who she could find to fix it before the next vacation season. Maybe get someone to landscape the overgrown yard. The way she saw it, she was already in trouble for paying off Sarah's mortgage. She might as well dig herself in a little deeper.

Ignoring the icy wood and the frigid wind, Jazz lowered herself onto the end of the dock, letting her feet hang over the edge. The lake was peaceful this time of the day, silent as the sun rose to bathe it in gold. In a few hours, she'd have to get to work, calling for the security system, calling around for a handyman, bringing Sarah to breakfast and to the doctor. Right now, though, all that she needed to do was sit and listen to the quiet.

Her fingers traced the weathered wood at the end of the dock, unconsciously searching for the deep indentations she knew would still be there, her mind drifting to another time, to bright sunlight and excited giggles, to the deep rumble of John's laughter. Her heart yearned to rewind the clock, go back and live those moments one more time.

"It's not such a good morning to be on the lake." The words were as soft as a butterfly's kiss, but still loud enough to make Jazz jump.

She turned, saw Eli walking toward her—his long legs and broad shoulders making him look like some action hero come to life—and felt something stirring to life. Interest? Attraction? Whatever it was, she didn't like it, and scrambled to her feet to face the man. "You're out and about early."

"Seemed a shame to waste any of the day." His deep Southern drawl washed over her, inviting her to relax into the moment as he moved closer.

She took a step back, one foot slipping off the edge of the dock, her arms windmilling as she tried to regain her balance.

Eli grabbed her hand, yanking her toward him, then holding her steady. "You okay?"

"Dandy." She tugged her hand away, resisting the urge to wipe it against her jeans. There was no way, after all, that she could wipe away the lingering heat of his touch.

"You look awfully tired for someone who's feeling dandy."

"Nice of you to notice."

"I also noticed that your eyes are more green than blue this morning and that your cheeks are the color of Gran's prize roses—the most delicate shade of pink I've ever seen—but I figured you'd be none too happy if I mentioned it."

Despite herself, she smiled. "Did you go to school to learn lines like that, or do they just come naturally?"

"Depends on who you talk to. I'd like to say I'm just naturally charming. Gran would probably say she whipped gentlemanly charm into me."

"Did I say I found you charming?"

"Don't you?" He smiled and the warmth of it spread through Jazz, melting ice that had surrounded her heart for three years, the feel of it new and exciting and horrifying all at the same time.

She looked away, told herself she was imagining things. "Maybe we better get off the dock. It needs some maintenance."

"I was thinking the same." Before she could move past, Eli wrapped a hand around her elbow, escorting her off the dock and back toward the house, the gesture courtly and charming. "You didn't tell me why you look so tired this morning."

"You didn't ask."

"So now I am."

"Sarah nearly screaming the house down, the sheriff's visit and tea with a stranger didn't leave me much time for sleep."

"Now, I wouldn't say we were strangers."

"I wouldn't say we were friends either."

"Maybe we will be." He smiled again, but this time his eyes were sharply focused and Jazz caught a glimpse of the hardness she'd seen in his gaze the day before.

Southern charm and warm smile aside, Jazz was pretty

sure Eli had an agenda. One that wasn't as simple as spending a month alone writing, as he'd claimed when he'd made reservations. "I doubt either of us will be here long enough for that to happen."

"It doesn't take long for friendships to form."

"I guess you've traveled around enough to know that."

"I sure have." He grinned, but it didn't ease the hard angle of his jaw.

"Last night, you said you'd been in the marines."

"That's right."

"And that you're retired."

"That's right."

"You didn't say how you went from military to writing."

"You didn't ask." His amusement was obvious. It might have been directed at her, at himself, or at the situation they were in. Probably, he was just the kind of guy who was amused by most things. The immature, unreliable type that Jazz's mother had always been attracted to.

Even as Jazz told herself that, she knew it wasn't the truth. There was something very solid about Eli, something that begged to be relied on. Not by her, of course. She had no intention of relying on anyone but herself. That would be asking for heartbreak and Jazz had definitely had enough of that to last a lifetime. "So, I'm asking. How does a person go from a military career to a writing career?"

"He gets half-near killed by a roadside bomb, gets shipped home, nearly goes crazy thinking about the good…no, the great…guys who died that day and then he decides he'd better find something edifying to do with his time, or he'll end up wandering the streets with a bottle of whiskey in his hand." He said it so matter-of-factly Jazz almost didn't register the horror of the words.

"I'm sorry. I didn't realize…"

"How could you have? My scars are pretty well hidden."

"I'm still sorry."

"It was a tough time, but I'm healing." They were still walking, Eli's arm brushing hers. Despite the poignant story Eli was telling, it felt nice to share the moment with him. Dawn had always been her favorite time of day, and she'd much rather spend it with a flesh-and-blood man than with a memory. Maybe she shouldn't feel guilty about that, but she did.

She shoved the emotion to the back of her mind, not wanting to dwell on it, and turned her attention to the conversation. "What kind of writing do you do?"

"Human-interest stories. Mostly about injured veterans who've returned from the war and made something of themselves. Men and women who haven't just survived, but thrived."

"And you came to Lakeview to write a story?"

He hesitated, and she knew before he spoke that he wasn't going to tell her the truth. "I'm researching."

"That could mean a lot of things."

"It could." Before she could question him more, he released her elbow, stepped away. "It looks like we've made it back to the house. I'd invite myself in for tea, but I'm more a coffee kind of guy in the morning."

She almost invited him in. *Almost*. Then common sense and the need for self-preservation prevailed, and she nodded. "Have a good day, Eli."

"You, too."

She started up the porch stairs, but was pulled up short by his hand on her arm. "If you have any more trouble, you know where to find me."

"We won't."

"I wouldn't be too sure of that, Jasmine. Your mother-in-law is a pretty savvy lady. If she thinks she's in danger, she probably is."

"I hope you're wrong about that."

"Until you know for sure, be careful. A woman went missing in the next town over a couple of months ago. I'd hate for the same to happen to you or Sarah."

Jasmine went cold at his words. She'd thought Sarah's claims of danger exaggerated. At least she'd hoped they were. But if a woman had disappeared, maybe there was more to Sarah's claims than she'd thought. "What woman?"

"Her name was Rebecca McKenna."

"I've never heard of her."

"She hasn't made the news, but she *is* missing. Her brother hasn't heard from her in two months. He's not sure he ever will again." He let the words hang in the air before releasing her arm and stepping away. "Get a security system, Jasmine. Make sure you keep it on. I don't think I need to tell you what an ugly world this can be."

Before she could comment, he strode away, moving across the lawn and down to the driveway that led to his rental, leaving Jazz alone in the still morning air, his words whispering through her head. *I don't think I need to tell you what an ugly world this can be.*

No, he didn't need to tell her.

She knew.

And she'd do everything she could to make sure that ugliness didn't touch her or her mother-in-law again.

FIVE

"You are *not* paying for the security system, Jasmine. If I can't afford it on my own, I don't need it." Sarah's clipped tone matched the scowl on her too-pale face, and Jazz had a feeling nothing she said could change her mother-in-law's mind.

Of course, being as hardheaded as Sarah, she had to keep trying. "You do need it. And I can afford it, so we've got no problem."

"We've got a big problem, and that problem is that you're treating me like a child. Which I'm not. I'm an adult. Plenty capable of making my own decisions and paying my own way in the world." Sarah pushed open the car door.

"Hold on, Sarah. Let me get the walker out of the trunk."

"I'll make it to the house without the walker."

"The doctor said—"

"I don't care what the doctor said. I'm fine. As a matter of fact, I'm pretty sure I could dance a jig if I wanted to." She eased to her feet, but didn't move away from the car as Jasmine grabbed the walker from the trunk. Between the late night and the doctor's appointment, Sarah was looking worse for the wear, her deeply set eyes hollow in the early afternoon light, her mouth bracketed with lines that hadn't been there three years ago.

Worry beat a throbbing pulse at the base of Jasmine's neck, and she rubbed her hand against the ache as she handed Sarah the walker. "A jig, huh?"

Sarah smiled and shrugged, some of the irritation easing from her face. "It might be interesting to try."

"It won't be long before you can."

"And it won't be long before you're heading back to New Hampshire."

"I'll stay as long as you need me."

"I know you will, dear, but my point is that eventually you'll go back to your life and I'll go back to mine because we're both *adults*. You don't need to worry about me. I'm perfectly capable of taking care of myself and my problems."

They were back to the security-system discussion. Not exactly the direction Jazz had hoped to go. The more they talked about money—most specifically, Sarah's lack of it—the more Jazz realized just how upset her mother-in-law was going to be when she found out the mortgage to her property had been paid off. Obviously, Jazz should have prayed more and taken a few days to think things through.

She hadn't, so she'd just have to face up to Sarah's wrath. But not now. They were both too tired for more arguments. "I know that, Sarah, but I want to help. You're the only family I've got, and I want to make sure you're safe."

To her credit, Sarah didn't bring up the fact that Jasmine had barely had contact with her during the past few years. "We'll see what the security people say, okay? Once we know for sure how much it will cost to have a system installed, we'll talk about it again."

"I'd really like it to be installed today. Eli said a woman is missing. Someone from a nearby town. That makes me nervous for your safety."

"What woman? I haven't heard anything about this."

"You were in the hospital for almost two weeks."

"And you think the rumor mill couldn't find me there? If someone was missing, I'd know about it."

"Eli seemed pretty sure about it."

"Who? Did he give you a name?"

"Rachel… Rebecca… Something like that."

"Rebecca McKenna?"

"Yes. That was it."

"She didn't disappear. She left her husband. I can't say I blame her. Reverend McKenna is a hard man with very antiquated ideas about the role of women in the home and in the church."

"*Antiquated* as in traditional?"

"Tradition is good. Reverend McKenna's approach is a little too extreme for my taste, and for the taste of most women I know."

"You've been to his church?"

"I've *heard* about his church. You know how the grapevine works around here. Rumor on top of rumor on top of rumor passed from person to person, but always with a grain of truth. According to the people I've talked to about it, Fellowship Community Church is more a cult than anything else. But, like I said, I've never been."

"If all you've got is rumor to go on, it's possible Rebecca didn't leave her husband. Maybe she really did disappear."

"I doubt it. One of the girls who helped out around here for a while said Rebecca ran off with someone she'd met while she was taking classes at Liberty University. Mary was a member of the church, so I think she probably knew what she was talking about." Sarah unlocked the front door and stepped into the house, her shoulders bowed as if a weight were sitting on them. And not just one weight. Many. The weight of disappointment. The weight of sorrow. The weight of financial difficulties.

Jazz wanted to put a hand on Sarah's shoulder and tell her that everything was going to be all right, but she knew it might not be. That was the thing about life. You'd get moving along, everything going well, and suddenly the rug would be yanked out from under you and you'd find yourself flat on your back, staring at the ceiling and wondering how you'd gotten there. "I guess Eli got some wrong information."

"That's what it sounds like. Either that, or everyone else does. Maybe you should discuss it with Eli over dinner or a movie. Or both." Sarah shot Jazz an amused look as she lowered herself onto the couch.

Jazz ignored the look and the comment. There was no way she was going to seek Eli out, let alone have dinner with him. Besides, Rebecca had probably done just what the rumor mills were saying and run off with another man. "It's past noon. How about some lunch? I could make soup and sandwiches while we wait for the security company to get here."

"I'm not hungry, dear. I think I'll just read for a while."

"Maybe you could just have some soup."

"You're doing it again." Sarah grabbed a paperback from the side table.

"What?"

"Treating me like a child."

"Sorry."

"It's okay." Sarah smiled John's smile again, and Jasmine turned away, grabbing a pile of books that lay on the coffee table and placing them on the bookcase. All around her there were reminders of the past, of the simple rhythm of life before. Before John and the girls had been killed, before she understood what true grief was, before she realized that a heart could be torn in two and still go on beating. It could. It did. And she had no choice but to keep living, to keep doing her best to find the path she was supposed to travel.

Whatever that might be.

She sighed, walking down the hall and into her room, wishing she had the kind of faith that would make her feel as if something good would eventually come of her loss. She knew it was what she was supposed to believe; it was even what she wanted to believe. She just wasn't sure she did believe it. How could good come from losing the only man she'd ever loved? How could it come from losing the children she would have given her own life to save?

"Faith needs to be a little easier, Lord. A little more concrete. Not feelings and emotions and hunches, but firmly grounded facts." She snatched the sketch pad from the desk, but couldn't focus enough to do any drawing. She'd known coming to Lakeview would be difficult, but she'd thought she was far enough away from the tragedy and her grief not to let the memories get to her. Apparently she'd been wrong.

The doorbell rang, and she hurried back toward the living room, motioning for Sarah to relax back down onto the sofa she was struggling up from. "I'll get it. It's probably the security company."

"Just remember, you're not paying for the system to be installed."

Jazz ignored the comment as she pulled open the door. She expected to see a uniformed representative of A-plus Security Systems; maybe an older man carrying a clipboard and a DVD featuring underpaid actors telling tales of break-in horrors.

That was what she expected to see. What she actually saw was Eli. Standing in the shadow of the porch, backlit by watery sunlight, he looked dark and dangerous. More like the man she'd met at the cabin the previous day than the charming, easygoing guy she'd spoken to that morning. The dichotomy bothered her. Who was he, really? "Eli. What can I do for you this afternoon?"

"I was hoping to speak with Sarah."

"About?"

"No need to screen my visitors, dear. Come on in, Eli," Sarah called out from the living room, and Jasmine's cheeks heated.

Eli shot a half smile in her direction before moving past, the scent of him tickling her nose as he stepped into the house—spicy, masculine. Compelling.

Her heart jumped and a million butterflies danced in her stomach. She didn't like it. She should not be having this kind of reaction to the man. She *would not* have this kind of reaction to him.

She took a deep breath and followed Eli into the living room. He'd already taken a seat on the recliner and was leaning toward Sarah, his elbows on his knees, his golden eyes focused on her. If he noticed that Jazz had stepped up beside him, he didn't acknowledge it. She had a feeling, though, that he *had* noticed. She was pretty sure there wasn't much he missed.

"Sorry for dropping by uninvited, Sarah."

"There's no need to apologize. I'm always glad to have visitors." Sarah smiled at him as if he were a Publishers Clearing House representative offering her a giant-sized check, her eyes sparkling for the first time since Jazz had arrived in town.

"Thanks. I had a few questions I wanted to ask if you don't mind."

"About the rental? Is everything okay with the cabin?"

"The cabin is fine. It's probably the best accommodations I've had all year."

"I'm glad. So, what *did* you want to ask about?"

"A young lady named Mary Cornell. I heard she worked for you until a couple of months ago. Is that true?"

At his words, Sarah stiffened. Not much, but enough for Jazz to notice. She tensed, too, curious and somehow anxious though she wasn't sure why.

"Yes, it is. She worked here for six months." Sarah leaned back in her seat, and Jazz was sure she was doing her best to look relaxed and unconcerned. It wasn't working. Tension rolled off her, filling the room and demanding attention.

"She quit a few months ago?"

"Six or seven weeks ago, I think. I hired another college student a few days later."

"Did Mary give you a reason for quitting?"

Sarah hesitated for a heartbeat, just long enough for Jazz to notice. "No."

It was a lie. Jasmine knew her mother-in-law well enough to recognize the tightness in her jaw, the frown line between her brows. What was she hiding and why was she hiding it? Curious, Jasmine took a seat in the old rocking chair that sat beside the recliner. The rocking chair she'd rocked the girls to sleep in. The one she hadn't had the heart to give away to anyone but family.

The time-worn wood of the armrest felt warm beneath her suddenly chilled fingers, and she clutched it tight as if that could anchor her in the present.

"I spoke to Mary's pastor earlier. He said she left seven weeks ago. Her parents haven't seen her since."

"That's a shame." Sarah's response was noncommittal, and Jazz was sure she knew a lot more about Mary than she was letting on.

"Yeah, her mom is pretty broken up about it." Eli paused, his gaze sharply focused. "Her father thinks you might know something. According to the pastor, he seems pretty convinced that you know where his daughter is. That you might even have helped her leave."

Sarah blanched, but she didn't look away. "Maybe if Jackson Cornell had been as interested in helping his daughter pursue her dreams as he is in making accusations, Mary wouldn't have felt the need to run away."

"So she was running away from her father?"

"I don't know her reasons, but I do know that things weren't easy at home. Her parents and that hardnosed pastor of theirs didn't agree with her plans to attend college. They wanted her to marry right out of high school. It was ludicrous."

"Lots of people do that, Sarah."

"Of course they do. *I* did. But I was in love. Mary wasn't."

"It sounds like you know a lot about her."

"That doesn't mean I know where she is, if that's what you're wondering."

"I was. I need to speak with her about Rebecca McKenna."

"Rebecca fell out of love with her husband and in love with a man she met at Liberty University. It's as simple as that."

"Maybe so, Sarah, or maybe not. Until I find Rebecca, I can't know for sure what happened."

"And I suppose there is a reason you need to find her?"

"I'm doing a favor for a friend. Someone still in Iraq. He asked me to find his sister and make sure she's okay."

"Then I wish I could help you, but Mary's the one who told me Rebecca ran off with another man. I doubt she has anything else to add to the story."

"I'd still like to speak with her. Do you know how I can get in touch with her?"

There was another minute hesitation before Sarah spoke. She was going to lie again. Jasmine knew it as well as she knew her own name.

"No."

"You're sure?"

"Young man, I may be recovering from hip surgery, but I

assure you there is nothing wrong with my brain. I'm very sure that I can't help you get in touch with Mary."

Did Eli notice the odd phrasing of Sarah's response? Jazz dared a quick look in his direction, saw the tightness of his jaw and the frown that added more than a hint of danger to his hard-angled face. "A woman is missing. If you know anything—"

"She already said she doesn't," Jazz cut in, then wished she hadn't as Eli leveled the full force of his gaze on her.

"Sometimes things we don't think are significant are very important."

"Sarah either knows how to get in touch with Mary or she doesn't. She says she doesn't." It might not be the truth, but Jasmine had to assume Sarah had good reason for her subterfuge.

"Since you two seem to be doing quite well having this conversation without me, I think I'll go lie down. Maybe a little rest will strengthen my feeble memory." Sarah smiled as she rose to her feet, but her face was drawn, her eyes shadowed.

"I appreciate your time, Sarah, and I hope you know I wasn't implying—"

"That I'm a feeble-minded old lady?" Sarah arched a brow, and Jasmine was reminded of years gone by. Years when she'd been a teenager dating a handsome first-year college student, years when she'd been newly married and unsure, years when one raised eyebrow from Sarah would make her cringe and run for cover.

Eli seemed to take the look and her comment in stride, his tone never changing as he rose and offered Sarah a quick, warm smile. "You're far from old and definitely not feeble minded."

"Then you're welcome to my time. Stop by again another day. For now, I really do need to rest."

"I'll see you again soon, Sarah." The words were a promise, or maybe a threat. Jasmine wasn't sure, and staring into Eli's eyes didn't clarify things. Shadows shifted in their depths—first deep gold, then brown, then vibrant green.

Sarah didn't seem to notice. She was already on her way down the hall, her salt-and-pepper curls lank and lifeless. Jasmine really needed to bring her to the hairdresser. Sarah had always said she felt more herself when her hair and nails were done. Unfortunately, broaching the subject would just cause another heated discussion about finances since Sarah didn't currently have enough cash to pay for a salon treatment.

"You're pensive."

Jasmine met Eli's gaze, her heart jumping in acknowledgment. What was it about him that threw her off-kilter? Made her want to take a second, third, even a fourth look? He was handsome, sure, but there was something else, something intangible that seemed to demand her attention no matter how much she didn't want it to. "I'm just worried about Sarah. She hasn't been herself."

"It's hard when you're used to being independent and suddenly have to rely on others for all your needs."

"I guess you've been there."

"Sure have, and I wasn't happy about it." Eli walked to the front door, pushing it open and letting in a blast of winter air. "Eventually, though, I got better, got my strength back a little at a time until I was independent again. Sarah will do the same, so don't worry too much about her."

"I can't help it. She's all the family I have left."

"Worry won't get you anywhere, Jasmine. Put your effort into something else. Like getting that security system installed."

"We've got a guy coming out this afternoon."

"Glad to hear it. That'll save *me* from worrying."

"You don't need to worry about us, Eli."

"Sure I do. We're neighbors after all." He smiled, his voice like hot chocolate on a cold day, sliding along her spine, warming her.

Surprised, she stepped back, knocked into the wall and the picture that hung there. It clanked against drywall, swung sideways.

"Whoa! Be careful. I don't think Sarah will be happy if that ends up on the floor." Eli reached past her shoulder, stopping the still-swaying photo. Then leaning forward to take a closer look.

Jasmine glanced back, knowing what she would see, but compelled to look anyway. John, Maddie, Megan and Sarah. On the dock hugging each other close, smiling as Jasmine laughed and snapped one picture after another, the sunlight fading behind her family and turning the golden afternoon to purple dusk. A long-ago day of happiness. A memory she wanted to hold on to as much as she wanted to let it go.

"Nice family." Eli was still studying the photograph, his hazel eyes scanning each face as if he could read the story there.

"Yes. They were." Jasmine sidled past, stepping out onto the porch and letting the crisp winter air cool her cheeks and force back the memories. Life was what it was. She needed to live it, not dwell in the past.

She took a deep breath of the cool air, feeling rather than hearing Eli step up behind her.

"Everything okay?"

"Fine. I just needed some fresh air." She turned to face him, bracing herself for the attraction she felt whenever she looked in his eyes. "And I didn't want Sarah to hear what I need to say to you."

"That doesn't sound good."

"It's not bad either." She took another lungful of winter air, letting the crisp coldness of it bolster her. "I want to know exactly who you are, why you're here, and what you want from Sarah." She expected Eli to shrug off her question, and was surprised when he nodded.

"Fair enough, if you'll do something for me."

"What?"

"Convince her to tell me where Mary is."

"She says she doesn't know."

"She's lying."

It was true. Jasmine knew her mother-in-law hadn't been telling the truth. What she needed to know was why. Maybe Eli could give her the answer to that. She had a feeling he knew a lot more about what was going on than she did. Whether or not he was trustworthy remained to be seen.

SIX

Eli waited for Jasmine's answer, his mind still back in the house, taking in the faces he'd seen in the photograph. Jasmine's daughters had looked like their mother—stunning even in their preadolescent years. Smiling into the camera with the open innocence of youth, they'd been coltish and thin in their shorts and T-shirts, their faces heart-shaped, their eyes bright blue rather than the green-blue of their mother, filled with humor and excitement, the world stretching out before them.

His stomach clenched with the truth of Jasmine and Sarah's loss. So much heartache, and yet the two women continued on, moving forward despite the pain. Not everyone could do that. The fact that they had, reaffirmed what he'd already known—the Hart women were strong.

Maybe not strong enough to deal with whatever was happening, though. Maybe this time they'd need someone besides themselves. Maybe he could be that person. Or maybe he should just walk away.

"I can't agree to help you get information about Mary until I know what's going on." Jasmine's words pulled him from his thoughts, and he looked down into her eyes. There were shadows there. And memories.

"Everything I told Sarah is true. I've got a good friend over in Iraq. The last time he heard from his sister was two months ago. He's worried."

"So you just agreed to come look for her?"

"He saved my life. I owe him." Marcus had pulled Eli from the rubble and tied a tourniquet around his thigh, stopping the blood pulsing from his femoral artery. A few weeks searching for his missing sister wasn't nearly enough to repay the debt.

"Has your friend contacted the police?"

"He has. They questioned Rebecca's husband. He claims she packed her bags and left while he was away at a men's retreat. Says she left a note. Signed and everything. The police have no reason to doubt him, and no evidence to the contrary."

"Convenient."

"Yeah, isn't it?" He leaned a hip against the porch railing, studying Jasmine's face as she stared out toward the lake. There were deep hollows beneath her cheekbones, dark circles under her eyes, but aside from those things she looked closer to twenty-five than thirty-five, her skin silky smooth and unlined despite the devastating loss she'd suffered. It was her eyes that gave away her sorrow. Dark, haunted, filled with shadows.

"You're staring." She turned to face him, and he caught his breath at the simple beauty he saw in her face.

"That's because I see something different every time I look at you."

"Should I ask what?" She smiled, but the worry in her gaze was unmistakable. Obviously, she was uncomfortable with his attention.

"Fragility. Strength. Beauty."

"Beauty? I don't know who you're looking at, but it's not

me." She shifted her gaze back to the lake, cutting off any further comments he might have made. "Sarah's been through a lot the past few weeks. She needs to rest and heal, but I'll try to get her to talk about Mary. See if she can give me any more information."

"Try hard. Sarah's secrets may be dangerous."

"You can't be serious."

"Someone pushed her down the steps. Someone was staring in the window at her."

"And you think it has something to do with Rebecca and Mary?"

"I think that it pays to be cautious."

"Caution is one thing. Paranoia is another. This is real life, Eli, not some story you're writing. People aren't running around Lakeview knocking each other off and hiding the crimes."

"Are you willing to risk your mother-in-law's life on that assumption?"

"You know I'm not." She frowned, her eyes flashing.

"Then do everything you can to get an answer from Sarah. The sooner I find Mary, the better off we'll all be."

"Maybe."

"Probably." He walked down the porch stairs, hoping he was right and that finding Mary would lead to answers about Rebecca.

"Sarah may not be willing to tell me anything." Jasmine hurried down the steps, following Eli into the yard and not sure why.

He glanced over his shoulder, his eyes golden-green in the afternoon light, his jaw tight with tension. He looked like a fighter, a soldier. "I'll keep searching for answers, one way or another. My friend deserves to know what happened to his sister."

"I know. And I really will try to help."

"Thanks. Now go on inside and lock the doors. You never know who could be lurking around here."

"You're very good at giving me new things to worry about. You know that?"

"I'm also very good at keeping people safe, but only if they let me."

"If you're talking about Sarah and me, we can take care of ourselves."

"I'm sure you can, but sometimes it's good to have someone else along for the ride." He brushed a strand of hair away from her cheek, leaned in close to stare into her eyes. Gold, green, brown; his eyes were a hodgepodge of colors that made her want to keep looking, keep exploring.

She wanted to move away, but she was frozen in place, fascinated and not sure why. There'd been men in her life since John. Men who'd been just as handsome, just as charming. She hadn't given them a second look.

She shook her head, trying to free herself from whatever spell he'd woven. "Sometimes, but not this time."

"No? The way I see it, God puts people into our lives for a reason."

She laughed, more from nerves than amusement. "So, God put you in our lives to protect us?"

"Could be. Or it could be He put you in my life so I could find the answers Marcus needs."

"I guess you've got an easy way to figure out which one is the truth."

"Why does it need to be one or the other? Why can't it be both? Or all three?"

"Three? We've only mentioned two possibilities."

"True, but it could be there's another." His slow smile warmed her heart, made her want to smile back.

Not good. Not good at all.

A white security-company van barreled up the driveway and a man stepped out, hurrying up the stairs to the front door and saving Jasmine from having to comment. "I've got to go. Sarah will send the security people away if I'm not there to stop her."

"She doesn't want a security system?"

"She doesn't want me to pay for it. Unfortunately, there's no other choice."

"Tough times at Lakeview Retreat?"

"For now, but things will be better soon." She hoped.

As Jasmine rushed toward the house, she shoved thoughts of Eli to the back of her mind.

He was a man, not some divine appointment from God. As far as Jasmine was concerned, the sooner she got information about Mary and was able to send him on his way, the happier she'd be.

And if she kept telling herself that, she just might believe it.

She sighed, coming up the porch steps just as the security-company representative was heading away from the front door, a scowl on his broad, round face.

"Hi, I'm Jasmine Hart. I'm glad you could come on such short notice."

"That's not what the other Mrs. Hart said." His dark eyes flashed with irritation. "She said there'd been a mistake and you don't need a system installed."

"She was wrong. We definitely need the system. Come back inside and we'll discuss it."

"Look, lady, I'm not into wasting time. I've got other people waiting and if you're not really interested, I'd just as soon not discuss anything."

"We are. Really. I absolutely guarantee that we're going to be purchasing a security system from you today."

Mollified, he nodded and started back up the steps.

Jasmine followed a little more slowly, not anxious to face Sarah's stubbornness. It had been a rough morning. Obviously the afternoon wasn't going to be any better.

She stepped into the house, started to close the door and caught sight of Eli. He was standing near the van, relaxed and at ease, but watchful, his gaze intense and focused. What was he looking for? What was he expecting would happen?

Goose bumps rose on her arms, and she closed the door, fear chasing her into the living room and the debate that had already begun.

SEVEN

It took two hours to convince Sarah that a security system was necessary regardless of the cost. Another hour and a half for the system to be installed. Windows. Doors. Every conceivable point of entrance was now being monitored. Jasmine was relieved. Sarah was less than happy and made her thoughts known as Jasmine pan-fried fish and prepared a salad.

"That man took you for a ride. No way do we need an alarm on that tiny window in the bathroom. It's so small even you couldn't get in. Why waste money on it?"

"Better safe than sorry."

"And just how many times did he say that? So many that I wanted to write the words down on a piece of paper and shove it in his mouth just to keep him from repeating them for the millionth time."

"Sarah!" Surprised, Jasmine shot her mother-in-law a hard look. "I can't believe you just said that."

"Believe it. It's amazing how having a murderer after me has changed my perspective on what is acceptable and what's not."

"If you're so sure that a murderer is after you, you shouldn't be complaining about the security system."

"Of course I should. I've been paying my own way in this

world since my husband died. I raised John without help from anyone. I don't plan on taking handouts now that I'm an old lady, and I'm especially not happy about taking them from you."

"It isn't a handout when it's family. It's a gift." Jasmine turned her attention back to the salad, hoping her mother-in-law wouldn't notice the sudden color in her cheeks. She really needed to tell Sarah the truth about what she'd done with the mortgage, she just wasn't sure how to broach the subject.

Okay. She was sure. She just didn't want to. Yet.

"It *is* a handout. And I'm going to pay you back. Every cent. Once spring comes, this place will fill up and I'll have plenty of spare cash."

"Exactly. So there's no need to worry about paying me back until then." Jasmine set a plate of food in front of Sarah, then took a seat across the table from her. She might not want to discuss paying off the mortgage, but she did want to discuss Mary. The sooner she found out what was going on, the better she'd feel. "I've been thinking."

"About?"

"About what Eli said."

"He said quite a few things."

"He said he wonders if Mary knows something about Rebecca's disappearance. I can't help but think she might. After all, it does seem strange that both women disappeared at the same time."

"I wouldn't say it was the same time, and I already told you Rebecca didn't disappear."

"What about Mary? She was young, right?"

"Eighteen. Old enough to make up her own mind about what she wanted to do and where she wanted to be."

"Did she mention where that might be?"

"I already told Eli that I can't tell him anything about Mary."

"That's a lot different than not knowing anything."

"Is it?"

"You know it is. So do I. So did Eli. You've never been very good at lying."

"Which is why I'm not lying now." Sarah took a bite of fish. "Very good dinner by the way. It will be even better if we change the subject."

"Sarah, I really wish…" What did she wish? That Sarah would trust her enough to tell her what was going on? That the last few years hadn't passed almost silently between them? That the relationship they'd once had hadn't turned awkward? "You're right. Let's change the subject. What do you want to do tomorrow?"

"Besides church, you mean?"

Church. Of course, tomorrow was Sunday. Where else would Sarah want to be? Personally, Jasmine would rather be *anywhere* else. When she was at home, she forced herself to attend. Anything to keep busy. But her home church was large and easy to hide in. Besides, people there didn't know anything about her or the tragedy she'd lived through. "After church."

"I'd like to visit my friend Myrna if it's not too much trouble for you to drive me there. She's in Bedford. About twenty minutes from here."

"Of course it's no trouble."

"While I'm there, maybe you could run to Wal-Mart and price some curtains. I think it's time to spruce up the cabins, update them a little for the spring season."

"Sure. I can do that."

"Wonderful. Other than those things, I can't think of much I'd like to do."

"Let me know if you do. I'm happy to do whatever you want."

Sarah nodded, seemingly satisfied to let the conversation wane, grabbing her paperback from the middle of the table and reading while she finished her meal. Jasmine picked at her own food, her stomach churning with anxiety and frustration. The house used to be so noisy, so filled with life. Now it was a dead thing, decaying from the inside out.

She stood abruptly, putting her plate into the sink. "I think I'll go for a walk."

"It's dusk. Are you sure that's a good idea?"

"I'll be fine."

"What if someone is outside waiting for one of us to open the door?"

If Jasmine hadn't known better, she'd have laughed, thinking Sarah's question was a joke. It wasn't. Sarah's fear was almost palpable, wrapping claw-like fists around Jasmine's heart and making it beat a hard erratic rhythm.

Don't let yourself be pulled into this, Jazz. There's nothing out there.

Was there?

No, of course there wasn't.

Sarah's fear and Eli's warnings were doing a number on her mind, that was all. "No one is out there, Sarah. Besides, it's not even dark yet. If someone were really going to skulk around, wouldn't he wait until he was sure he couldn't be seen?"

"Just be careful, okay?"

"I will be." Jazz dropped a kiss on Sarah's cheek and left the room, grabbing her coat and pushing open the front door. Winter's icy breath rushed in, whipping Jasmine's cheeks and making her shiver. Maybe staying home wasn't such a bad idea.

She turned, saw one of the dozens of photographs Sarah had

displayed. Maddie this time. The quiet twin. Soft-spirited and easily wounded. Delicate in appearance and in emotion. Had she been afraid in those last moments of her life? Had she seen the car coming around the curve, felt the quick jerk of the wheel as John had tried to avoid the crash, known they were going over the edge of the mountain? Been awake and conscious as the car had soared into the air, dropped toward the earth?

The sour taste of despair flooded Jasmine's mouth, filled her throat, choking off air. She rushed into the cold, the freezing wind shaking her from the questions that had haunted her for years.

Questions that had no answers.

But she wanted answers. Wanted to know that her girls hadn't been afraid, that they hadn't suffered, that everything had happened too quickly for them to realize how far from home they were going.

Not far *from home*. Home.

Jazz could almost hear Maddie's voice, soft, gentle, trying to offer comfort. At seven, she'd understood so much more about life and death than her mother. She'd accepted with zeal the idea of God's perfect plan and timing. Her strong faith had only made Jazz's seem all the weaker.

Jazz rounded a curve in the driveway, suddenly realizing where she was heading. The old tree, its thick, strong branches fanning out over the lake. A swing hung from one fat limb, swaying in the wind, the chains that held it in place reddish-brown in the twilight. How many times had she come here with one of the girls or John, sat just so on the wooden bench seat, listened to the water lapping against rocks and earth?

The wood was weathered smooth from time and use, the soft creaking of the chains and the branch settling into silence as Jasmine shifted her weight and sat still.

Dreams. Hopes. Plans. Echoes of each filled her mind, and she let them come, let herself get lost for just a little while.

Eli knew he shouldn't have followed Jasmine, but he'd seen her walking and he'd been worried. There were a lot of things going on that he didn't understand. Undercurrents that were running through the Hart house and through the community. Two women gone, dropped off the face of the earth as if they'd never existed. He didn't want Jasmine to be the third.

Of course, if he were honest with himself, and he tried to be that, he'd admit that wasn't the only reason he'd followed her. The fact was he found Jasmine compelling. There was a story in her eyes, one about loss and grief and overcoming. It was a story he thought he could read over and over again. One he'd never get tired of.

Grass crackled under his feet as he moved toward the tree where Jasmine had disappeared. Dusk was already giving way to night, but he could still make out the wooden swing and the woman who sat there.

"Care for some company?"

She must have heard his approach, because she didn't jump at the sound of his voice, just motioned him over, her voice husky and soft in the darkness. "I hadn't planned on any, but I'm not opposed to it either."

"I guess that's just about the most ambivalent yes I've ever heard."

"I'm having an ambivalent night."

"As in not good, not bad?"

"As in I'm not sure if I want to be outside or in."

He lowered himself onto the bench, inhaled a subtle flowery scent, sensed Jasmine's tension and something else. Something so real he thought he could reach out and touch it. Sorrow. Rolling off her. Bowing her shoulders, painting her face in shades of darkness.

Were those tear tracks on her cheeks?

He reached out, brushed a hand down the soft, smooth flesh, felt the moisture, the warmth, and an unexpected zing of awareness. He dropped his hand, leaned in closer, could see the moisture still in her eyes. "You're crying."

"Everyone does sometimes."

"Usually for a reason."

"I've got one."

"Care to share?"

"No. No, I don't." She wiped her hand against the spot he'd touched, and he wondered if she felt the same awareness he had.

"Did I tell you I've got four sisters?"

Her brow furrowed at the change of subjects, but she went with it. "No. You didn't."

"Well, I do. Four sisters. All older than me. Between them, Mom and Gran, Dad and I were hopelessly outnumbered."

"I hope you had a lot of bathrooms in your house."

"Ah, you've hit on one of the downsides of having sisters. We only had two bathrooms and that wasn't nearly enough. Sometimes I'd give up waiting to get my turn and go to my best friend's house to use the bathroom. I'll tell you, it got to the point I was using their bathroom so much his mother threatened to charge me a fee."

She laughed softly, the sound carrying out onto the lake and drifting in the cold night air. "Smart lady."

"Would've been smarter if she'd actually followed through, but she always had a soft spot for me and I guess she just couldn't bring herself to do it."

"Why do I have a feeling most women you know have a soft spot for you?"

"Now that's up for debate. What I do know is this—being

raised around so many women has taught me a few things about crying. It's best to get the emotions out in the open. Holding them in will only make the wound fester."

"The wound has festered, healed and scarred over. That doesn't mean it still doesn't hurt sometimes." She stood, moving away from the tree, standing at the edge of the lake and staring out over the water.

"Is it memories that hurt you so much?"

She stiffened at the question. "Why do you ask?"

"I know your husband and daughters were killed in a car accident three years ago."

"Sarah told you?"

"I saw the pictures in her house. The ones of you and your family." He hedged around the question, not wanting to tell her about the private investigator who'd dug into her life. He doubted that was something Jasmine would be happy to know about.

"They died on their way home from here. Traveling at night through the Blue Ridge Mountains. A drunk driver plowed into them and their car went over the side of the mountain. This is the first time I've been back to the retreat since the accident." Her voice was hollow and old, her eyes glistening with tears and anger, a well of emotion that Eli knew she kept in check most of the time.

"Too many memories?"

"They're everywhere. Carved into the wood of the dock, smiling from every picture in every room in Sarah's house. Here, under the tree where we used to swing and dream." She laughed and the sound was as dry and scratchy as old bones. "You must think I'm crazy."

"I think you're a woman who's suffered more than her fair share of loss. And I think you're a lot stronger than most would be."

"You're wrong. I'm not strong at all." Her voice broke, and Eli pulled her into his arms, wrapping her in the kind of hug he'd given his sisters a thousand times—comforting, strong, warm. Only with Jasmine it felt different. It felt like more.

"Feeling grief doesn't make a person weak, Jasmine. It makes her human. Strength lies in the ability to move forward when everything you love is in the past. You're doing that."

"Eli—" Before she could finish, a siren split the air, echoing down from the small rancher.

"The security alarm! Sarah!" Jasmine shouted the words as she raced back toward the house, running full out, Eli sprinting up ahead, a slight limp marring his gait but not slowing him down.

A dark car was parked in the driveway, small, compact. One Jasmine hadn't seen before. Her heart thrummed so fast, she thought it would leap from her chest.

She shouldn't have left Sarah alone. If anything had happened to her, Jasmine would never forgive herself.

"Stay out here." Eli grabbed her arm, stopping her before she could fly up the porch stairs.

"No way."

He was already moving, shoving open the front door, ducking low as he rushed inside.

Stay out there?

It wasn't going to happen. Jasmine rushed up the stairs and followed him into the house.

EIGHT

She'd barely crossed the threshold when the alarm stopped abruptly, cutting off mid-shriek. Her ears were ringing, her legs were shaking and she could barely take in the scene before her. Eli—his face as hard as stone, his eyes golden spears. Sarah—white-faced and shaken, leaning against her walker. A second woman—gray-haired, pale-faced, her mouth opened in a silent O.

"Young man. You just scared fifteen years off my life. And let me tell you, I can't afford it." Sarah collapsed onto the sofa, and the other woman did the same.

"*You* can't afford it? I'm three years older than you. He nearly *killed* me."

"Yes, but I've been through surgery. That probably took a few years off, too. I'm fortunate I'm still breathing after losing so many more years from fright."

As Jazz listened to the banter, a memory surfaced—Sarah and Germaine Walker arguing over who had the most financial problems, who had the most aches and pains, whose children were causing the most worry. "Mrs. Walker?"

"Who else? Come give me a hug, dear. It's been too long." Germaine stood, enveloping Jasmine in Chanel No. 5.

"I take it we've got no emergency going on here?" Eli

spoke with dry humor, his expression easing, his good-old-boy charm working its way to the surface again as he offered his hand to Germaine and smiled in a way that must have made the widow's heart do the same dance Jasmine's did every time she looked into his eyes. "Ma'am, I'm Eli Jennings. I'm renting one of Sarah's cabins."

"I'm Germaine Walker. It's good to meet you. I've been worried about Sarah being out here on her own. It's a relief to know she's got someone around to help out if she needs it."

"*I'm* around to help." Jasmine felt obligated to speak up, though she doubted Germaine would be as impressed with her presence in the house as she was with Eli.

"Well, yes, dear. You are. But what will you do if some crazed killer shows up and tries to murder our Sarah? Smile sweetly and ask him to go away?"

Eli choked down a laugh, grinning when Jasmine shot him a hard glare that couldn't hide her amusement. Obviously, she knew Germaine Walker and wasn't offended by the woman's blunt manners. Eli wasn't offended, either. As a matter of fact, he figured he could use them to his advantage.

He took a seat in the easy chair, ignoring Jasmine's frown. "I'm always glad to lend a hand when necessary, Mrs. Walker. So if either Sarah or Jasmine need me, I'll come running."

"Good to hear, young man. There are so few men who would be willing to say the same."

"Do you live around here, Mrs. Walker?"

"About thirty minutes away. Close to Peaks of Otter, if you know it."

At her words, Eli's nerves jumped to life. "I sure do. I drove out there earlier today. It's beautiful there. The Blue Ridge Mountains are a stunning testimony to God's artistry."

Germaine beamed at his words, leaning forward, her broad face wreathed in a smile. "Yes, you're so right. That's one of the reasons I live there. What were you doing out my way? Taking photographs? Sarah said you're a writer."

"I am, but I was actually interviewing people."

"For a story?"

"I'm looking for a woman who's been missing for a couple months. Her brother is worried and asked me to see what I could find out."

"Rebecca McKenna." Germaine nearly shouted the name, and Eli held back a smile. This was the kind of person he needed to talk to. If there was information to be had aside from Reverend McKenna's practiced answers, it would be someone like Germaine who'd offer it.

"That's right. Do you know her?"

"Not as well as some, but from what I've heard—"

"Eli, I want to get some tea started. Would you mind giving me a hand?" Jasmine interrupted, her soft lips pulled into a scowl, wind-whipped curls shining golden-brown and soft-looking. The way Eli saw it, he'd be more than happy to lend Jasmine a hand with just about anything she needed.

"Sure."

"Nonsense. Jasmine can manage on her own, can't you, dear?" Germaine smiled sweetly, but there was a hint of steel in her gaze. She reminded Eli of an elementary schoolteacher, bubbly and fun unless she was crossed. Apparently, Jasmine had crossed her.

"I'm sure she can, but I'm happy to help out. You'll excuse me for just a moment, ladies?" He flashed Sarah and Germaine a smile, and followed Jasmine from the room.

They'd barely turned the corner into the kitchen when Jasmine rounded on him, her whisper carrying a hint of anger and a truckload of irritation. "What are you thinking? You can't pick information from some poor unsuspecting woman's mind."

"I'm not picking anything. Mrs. Walker is more than happy to tell me whatever she knows. And I really doubt she is poor or unsuspecting." He filled the kettle and set it on the stove, moving out of the way as Jasmine set four teacups onto the counter.

"She's lonely. She's desperate for conversation. You're taking advantage of that." Tea bags spilled from the canister Jasmine had dragged from the cupboard, dropping onto the counter and floor. She scooped them up, her cheeks flushed with frustration.

"Jasmine, you and I both know Mrs. Walker isn't lonely, naive or unwilling to talk. My guess is she spends half her day on the phone and the other half visiting friends, discussing a wide range of community subjects. So what's the real issue here?"

"It'll take all of sixty seconds for her to tell most of the populations of Lakeview and Peaks Of Otter that you're looking for Rebecca. If someone really did harm her, that person might not be so happy with your questions."

"You're worried about me." He grinned as Jasmine's cheeks deepened in color.

"I'm worried about Sarah."

"There's no need. The questions I'm asking aren't any different than the ones Marcus has been asking every time he can get in touch with the police or the reverend. The boat was rocked long before I got here. I don't think my questions will make things any worse."

"I hope you're right."

"Do you really think I'd do something that would put Sarah in more danger?" He put a hand on her shoulder, felt the tense muscles there.

"I don't know, Eli. How can I?" She poured boiling water over tea bags, refusing to meet his eyes.

"Then let me assure you that I wouldn't. It may be too late for Rebecca, but it's not for Sarah. I won't risk her life to find information about someone who may never come home."

She looked up at his words, her expression unreadable as she searched his face for the truth or for reassurance. He could offer her both, though he doubted she'd believe it. Jasmine had built a wall around herself, and he didn't think she'd want him trying to climb it.

Finally, she nodded, lifting two teacups, a frown pulling at the corners of her mouth. "Okay. But whatever you hear from Germaine, take it with a grain of salt. She's not always the most reliable source."

"Since she's the only source willing to talk, I'll have to try to weed out the truth from the fiction. Ready?" He grabbed two of the teacups and strode out into the living room.

Both women looked up as he came in, and he handed each a cup of tea. "Here you are, ladies. Sorry about the wait."

"We barely noticed." Mrs. Walker smiled up at him, her brown eyes sparkling with enthusiasm. "We were too busy talking about you."

"Saying only good things, I hope."

"We were wondering about your job. Sarah mentioned that you write, but isn't sure if you write books or articles. I'll need to know so I can fill the ladies in my book club in."

"I do freelance work for several magazines."

"Magazines! That *is* impressive. Sarah also mentioned you're a war veteran?"

"That's right." He wasn't sure where the conversation was headed, but he'd go with it. Eventually they'd get back to Rebecca.

"You're a very accomplished young man. Which is exactly what my daughter's best friend's cousin needs."

At her words, Eli nearly choked on the tea he'd started to swallow. "Who?"

"She's in town for a visit. Thirty years old, attractive. A little too skinny, but I guess that's the style nowadays."

"Look, Mrs. Walker, I—"

"If you have time, I'm sure she'd love to speak with you about your writing career. Maybe over dinner."

Jasmine let out an unladylike snort, and Eli met her eyes, saw the laughter dancing in their depths. "That sounds nice, but I'm interested in someone else, and it wouldn't feel right going out to dinner with another woman."

Jasmine's amusement faded, and she looked unsure, nervous, maybe a little scared.

"Are you? That's too bad, but I suppose it's only to be expected. A man like you must attract his fair share of women."

"I wouldn't say that, but, then, I've only got eyes for one."

"Oh, a romantic. Your lady friend is very lucky."

"I'm not sure she agrees." He purposely glanced at Jasmine again, smiling when her cheeks heated.

"Luckier than most. Men aren't like they used to be. No courtly manners, no desire to treasure and cherish their girl-friends and wives. Personally, I don't think any woman should settle for less than that." Her words were the perfect segue, and Eli took advantage of them.

"Was that what happened with Rebecca? She settled for less than what she should have and got tired of it?"

"That was a different situation entirely."

"How so?"

Mrs. Walker sat forward, her gaze darting around the room as if someone might be lurking in the corners waiting to steal whatever wisdom she was about to impart. "Well, rumor has it…and this is for your ears only…Reverend McKenna tried to beat poor Rebecca down, turn her into a meek, mousy woman who'd fulfill his every whim."

"And that didn't sit well with her?"

"If you know anything about Rebecca, you know that wasn't her style. She had no problem with submitting to her husband, but she expected they would be a team, working together to strengthen the church."

"You knew her well?"

"Actually, we only met once, but people who did know her have told me Rebecca got fed up with being a doormat. That's the only reason any of them can think of for what she did. After all, she had high moral values. Only a serious issue would drive her away from her marriage."

"So McKenna is a hard man."

"Hard? Try impossible to live with. You know he was married before, right?"

"His wife died from heart failure a few years back." The investigator Eli had hired had already provided the information, but it was good to get it from another person's perspective.

"That's what the doctors say, but talk to anyone around these parts and you'll hear something different. That poor woman couldn't give the reverend a child and he never let her forget it. Eventually, it wore her down and broke her heart. The way I see it, it's probably good that Rebecca left. She might have ended up the same way."

"You might be right about that, Mrs. Walker." He continued the conversation, but his mind was racing along with his heart, a million possibilities humming through him. There were plenty of poisons that could kill a person over the long or short term and some of those weren't easily detected. He needed to do some research, find out if the coroner had ordered an autopsy on McKenna's deceased wife.

"Might be? Of course I'm right. McKenna is a hard man with strange ideas. He shouldn't be leading one of God's houses."

"Unfortunately, there are plenty of other men in the same position."

"Isn't that the truth?" Germaine sighed and shook her head. "Enough of this maudlin talk. I came to cheer Sarah up. Not drag her down."

"You're not dragging me down. I'm enjoying the conversation. The house is much too quiet for my taste. And you know how much more pain a person feels when she's not distracted by friends and conversation."

"Absolutely. Last year, when I had surgery, I was desperate for company."

"Sarah, Ms. Germaine, I hope you don't mind, but Eli and I were in the middle of a walk when we heard the alarm. We'd probably better finish it now before it gets too late," Jasmine broke in, shooting Eli a look that said she had things she wanted to talk about. Things she didn't want to discuss in front of the other two women.

"You and Eli on a walk?" Germaine's eyes widened, her mouth opening in surprise. "Of course we don't mind. Do we, Sarah?"

"Not at all." Sarah smiled at Jasmine, sending her a look that Eli couldn't quite interpret.

"Great. I'll see you tomorrow at church, Mrs. Germaine." Jasmine hurried toward the front door, pulled it open and disappeared outside before Eli could put his teacup away and say goodbye to both women.

He stepped outside, saw her standing beneath the porch light, curly hair a wild halo around her sharply angled face, and felt his heart leap, his pulse jump. "What's up?"

"I was afraid the conversation was going to deteriorate into a discussion of surgeries and pain. They each love to one-up each other. I thought I'd save us both from the gory details."

"And here I thought you just wanted to spend some time alone with me." He chuckled when she frowned, and then grabbed her hand, ignoring her sudden tension as he led her down the steps. "Of course, now we're obligated to take that walk."

"But not together. You can head home. I'll just hang out near the dock for a few minutes. Then go back inside."

"And listen to another hour of health woes? I can't let you do it. How about we go to my place instead?"

"Your place?" Jasmine didn't exactly squeak the words, but her voice sure did rise in pitch.

"Don't sound so shocked. We're both adults. It's not even nine at night and we've got some business to take care of."

"Business? What business?"

"A little research on Reverend McKenna's first wife. She died of heart failure for sure, but I'm beginning to wonder if there was an underlying cause. One the doctors don't know about."

"Now wait just a minute!" She dug her heels in and Eli allowed himself to be pulled to a stop.

"What?"

"Don't give me those innocent good-old-boy eyes. You're trying to drag me into your search for Rebecca and Mary."

"If what happened to them has something to do with what's going on with Sarah, I thought you'd want to be part of figuring it out."

"Yes, but we're not sure there *is* a connection and I don't want to spend any more time with you than necessary." Her eyes widened when she said it, her hand covering her mouth. If it hadn't been so dark, Eli was sure he'd be watching her blush. "I'm sorry. I didn't mean that to come out the way it did."

"No need to apologize. I understand."

"Do you?" She started walking again, and Eli matched her pace.

"I make you uncomfortable." He went ahead and said what was on his mind. No sense beating around the bush with Jasmine. She was too tough to allow it even if she didn't like the truth.

"No you don't."

"Sure I do. I'm a man who's obviously attracted to you, but you've lost a lot and you're scared."

"That is *not* why I don't want to spend time with you."

"No? Then what *is* the reason?"

She was silent for several minutes, the quiet sounds of the lake filling the night as a chilly wind buffeted the water and land. When she spoke, the humor in her voice was unmistakable. "I *am* afraid of being in another relationship, but I've also got an obligation to Sarah. She's the only family I have left and she's my priority while I'm here. I can't go spending time with every Tom, Dick or Harry who comes along while she's at the house alone."

"No, you can't. But I'm not every Tom, Dick or Harry, and Sarah's not alone. Germaine is with her."

"Maybe you're right, but I don't like it."

"Like what?" He glanced down into her face, remembering the tears that had been so warm against his palm, the heat of despair that had been so real and fresh in her eyes. She'd tucked that away, hidden it well, but he could still sense it just below the surface.

"Any of it. You. Me. Us. Sarah. Two women gone. I came here to help my mother-in-law. I didn't expect all the rest."

"Life is full of unexpected things. We can run from them or we can face them."

"Lately it seems I'm pretty good at running."

"You won't run this time, though."

"No. I won't. I can't leave Sarah."

"So let's face whatever is happening together."

"As a team?"

"Why not?"

She hesitated, then shrugged. "All right. A team. For now."

Which left room for later, and somehow Eli had a feeling that was what they were going to have. He kept the thought to himself as they made their way to the cabin and started searching for clues about the former Mrs. McKenna.

NINE

Eli was attracted to her.

Jasmine couldn't get the thought out of her mind as he turned on his computer and searched for information about McKenna's first wife. She wasn't sure if she was horrified or intrigued by the thought. Three years and she hadn't been attracted to anyone enough to go on even one date. With Eli, she had a feeling that if she let herself she'd feel a lot more than attraction. She just wasn't sure she wanted to let herself. Caring about someone made a person vulnerable. Jasmine never wanted to be vulnerable again.

"Take a look at this." Eli dropped a bowl of chocolate drops on the table and slid a computer printout in front of her before easing into a chair.

Strong jaw darkened by a five o'clock shadow, face chiseled and hard, he looked like the hero of some action-thriller movie. Handsome, strong, and slightly dangerous. Jasmine tried not to notice how muscular his chest was beneath the dark T-shirt he wore. *Tried* not to, but failed miserably. The man must work out a lot to keep a physique like that.

Which was something she *shouldn't* be noticing.

She focused her attention on the sheaf of paper Eli had given her, doing her best to ignore the man across from her.

"You're going to have to spell this out for me, Eli. All I see is that Lily McKenna died from heart failure at a young age."

"After a year of on-and-off illness and several hospitalizations with no diagnosis."

"Stress on the heart from an underlying undiagnosed disease. It happens."

"Sure it does. And maybe Lily's death by itself *would* mean nothing. Add it to Rebecca and Mary's disappearance and you've got another story. All three women attended Fellowship Community Church. Two of them were married to the pastor. That doesn't seem suspicious to you?"

"Not if it doesn't to the police." She glanced at the papers again, saw the face of the deceased woman. She'd been young and smiling in the picture, but there was something in her eyes. A darkness that might have been sadness or fear.

"What?"

"She looks sad in her photo. Or scared. I can't decide which."

"You think?"

He came around the table, leaning over her shoulder, his hand cupping her neck as he stared down at the photograph. To Eli it was probably just a brotherly gesture born of years spent with his sisters. But it didn't feel brotherly to Jasmine; it felt exciting and new, like the first tulip after a harsh winter. She shoved the feeling down, determined to keep her focus where it should be. "Yes, I do. Of course, it's easier to read people when you see them in the flesh."

"Unfortunately, we can't do that, but I have a feeling your instincts are right on." His hand dropped away, and Jasmine released a breath she hadn't realized she was holding.

"Don't count on it. All the talk of death and disappearances is making me suspicious. I'm probably making something out of nothing."

"Good. That'll make you more careful." He said it almost absently as he lifted the paper and scanned it again. "I think I may just attend services at Fellowship Community tomorrow. Find out what people are saying about the late Mrs. McKenna's illness."

"Do you think they'll talk about it?"

"There's always one Germaine Walker in a group. I think someone will have something to say." He grinned and butterflies took flight in Jasmine's stomach. This was *not* good, but somehow she didn't think she could stop it.

"Just be careful. If McKenna is a killer—"

"I've dealt with a lot worse, Jasmine, so don't worry too much about me."

"I'm not worried." Much.

"Sure you are. And I appreciate it, but you just focus your energy on keeping track of Sarah. Speaking of which, I've got to get you back to her."

Jazz glanced at the clock and stood quickly. "I didn't realize how late it was getting."

"Me neither. Time passes too quickly when I'm with you."

Time passes too quickly when I'm with you?

Did he practice these lines?

Jasmine shook her head, smiling a little as she imagined all the women who'd probably fallen for Eli's charm.

"You should smile more often, Jasmine. You're stunning when you do." His voice stroked her nerves, warming her, inviting her to do what she'd said she couldn't—fall for him. Good thing she was immune to butterflies and sweet invitations or she might just find herself in a place she didn't want to be. Dependent, filled with love for someone, dreaming of a future spent with another person rather than alone.

She didn't meet his eyes as she sidled around him and headed for the door, her heart thrumming a warning she couldn't ignore. She could deny it all she wanted, but Eli affected her deeply. And that was not a good thing.

He put a hand on her arm, his fingers curling around her bicep then smoothing down to her wrist, spreading warmth as they went. "If I'd known you were going to go all quiet on me, I wouldn't have complimented you."

"I'm not going quiet."

"Sure you are. And you're about as tense as a tree-hooked fishing line. There's no need to be uncomfortable, though. I was just making an observation that every other man you've ever known has probably made."

Actually, the opposite was true. Before John, none of Jasmine's boyfriends had ever complimented her. But then, they'd been bottom-of-the-barrel scum. John had called her *beautiful* and *pretty*, but *stunning* hadn't been in his vocabulary. No way was she going to tell Mr. Charming that, though.

She tugged her arm away, continuing to the door and pulling it open. "We really do need to get out of here."

"Let's take my car. It'll be faster."

"I'd rather walk."

"Walking a mile in this bitter cold is something my thin Southern blood can't take. Of course, if you really feel the need to walk, I'll sacrifice my toes and fingers to escort you." He grinned and Jasmine felt her heart melt just a little more.

Maybe the ride *was* a better idea. At least it would shorten the amount of time she spent with him. "The car is fine since your wimpy Southern blood can't handle the walk."

"Now, I don't believe I said anything about being wimpy." He pulled open the door to his SUV and ushered Jasmine in, humor coloring his words.

"That's my take on it."

"Ah, well in that case, maybe we *should* walk so I can prove my masculinity."

"Sorry. I'm already in the car." And really, she was tired enough that driving was a better option than walking.

"Then I guess I'll have to prove it some other way."

"No need for that. I'll take your word for it."

He chuckled and closed the door, leaving her in the dark as he stepped around the car.

No doubt he was completely fine with the cold. After her earlier tears, he probably thought she was some delicate flower that needed protection from the elements.

She almost snorted at the thought. Delicate? Not hardly. She'd been raised by her mother in a fading neighborhood in Boston. Most of the time she'd been alone, taking care of herself while her mom had waited tables and tried to make enough money to pay the rent and keep food on the table. That kind of life taught a person to be tough quick. Maybe, though, marriage to John had softened her. *Love* had softened her, so that she had nearly been destroyed by life's harsh blows. Not again, though. Never again.

"All set?" Eli slid into the car, the spicy masculine scent of him filling the interior and making Jasmine wish things were different. That she could relax and enjoy his attention rather than fight against it.

"Yes."

"Then let's go."

It took barely a minute to drive the mile to Sarah's house, and Jasmine was glad for the quick journey. She needed to put distance between herself and Eli. The quicker that happened, the better.

As soon as he stopped the car, she hopped out, hurried toward the house, calling over her shoulder as she went. "Thanks for the ride."

"It took all of sixty seconds, but you're welcome." His

hand wrapped around hers, pulling her up short, his palm warm and calloused against her chilled flesh.

Memories flashed through her mind—the first time John had held her hand, the first time he'd touched her face, the first time they'd kissed. Each tiny gesture leading to the next until affection had turned to love and love had become commitment. Marriage. Children. Contentment.

She couldn't and wouldn't go there again, but she couldn't make herself pull away either. She'd missed the feeling of belonging that bloomed when hands touched.

"There you are!" Sarah pushed open the door before they made it up the porch steps.

Surprised, Jasmine jerked her hand from Eli's and hurried up to her mother-in-law. "You shouldn't be up, Sarah."

"Of course I should. Besides, Germaine and I were just leaving. I left you a note, but since you're here, there's no need to read it."

"A note?"

"About Sarah staying with me tonight." Germaine stepped outside, a duffel bag in her hand, her short hair spiking around her face.

"Staying...with you?" She was parroting words like an idiot, but couldn't seem to stop herself. How had Sarah gone from recovering surgery patient to social butterfly so quickly?

"Our women's Bible study group is having breakfast at my house before church. I'm making my grandmother's quiche. Really delicious. There's no way Sarah can miss out."

"I can drive her there in the morning."

"That would mean getting up extra early, and what's the sense in that when she can just as easily stay in my house, eat breakfast with the gang and ride to church with one of us?"

"I—" Don't want to be alone in the house with dozens

of photos of my husband and kids. She couldn't say that, so she smiled, took the duffel from Germaine's hand. "It sounds like fun."

"Oh, it will be. I'll bring her back after the service. That way you can spend the morning and afternoon getting some rest. You're looking a little peaked."

"Thanks." She muttered the word as she followed Germaine down to her car. "You two behave tonight. I don't want to get any calls from the police saying you're having a wild party and the neighbors are complaining."

"We'll be wild, but quiet." Germaine chuckled as she slid into the driver's seat.

Sarah moved more slowly, Eli shadowing her as she made her way to the car, then offering her a hand as she lowered herself into the seat. "Thank you, Eli. You're quite helpful to have around."

"If you ever meet my gran make sure you tell her that." He smiled. "You be careful tonight, Sarah."

"I will."

"No worries. I've got an alarm system and a gun. If someone tries to get in, I'll make him sorry he did."

Germaine with a gun? The idea wasn't comforting. Jasmine kept the thought to herself, waving as Germaine pulled down the driveway.

"Are you going to be all right here alone tonight?" Eli's voice made her jump, and she whirled to face him.

"Of course. We've got a state-of-the-art alarm system hooked up to every window and door. I'll be right as rain." She tried to make her voice light and cheerful, but knew she failed miserably.

"You know where I am if you need me."

"Of course."

"And you'll call if anything happens."

"Sure." But nothing was going to happen. Except that she was going to spend a restless night in a house full of memories. Tears filled her eyes and she blinked them away, hurrying up the porch stairs and into the house, not wanting Eli to see how uneasy she was. It was silly, after all, to be afraid of being alone. And she wasn't afraid. Not really. More like uncomfortable.

She said a quick goodbye to Eli, closing the door on the dark night. The house was silent as she locked the door, set the alarm, made her rounds, checking each window and door. Every room she entered was filled with memories. Like land mines, they were hidden from view and exploded suddenly when she sat in a chair, touched an object. Bittersweet. Haunting. There were times when she thought she caught a whiff of John's cologne, or heard the soft laughter of one of the girls. That was what longing could do—make you imagine what wasn't there. Because they weren't there. No matter how much her mind tried to conjure them. They were in Heaven, safe in God's arms. Wasn't that what every sympathy card said, what every well-meaning friend had whispered in her ear in the days and months following the accident?

In God's arms?

She'd rather think of ballerina Megan dancing at His feet, giggling with joy; picture Maddie playing violin, her nimble fingers moving with the passion that came from finally knowing what you've believed for so long was true; believe John was watching their daughters, his heart full to overflowing with contentment and peace as he stood in the presence of His Savoir.

That was what she'd rather believe, but she really didn't know for sure. Maybe they *were* all curled up safely in arms large enough to hold the world.

She sighed, moving through the living room, turning off

lights and picking up clutter as she went. Paperback books, cups, a plate from something Germaine and Sarah must have eaten while she'd been gone. The light in Sarah's room was on and she went in to turn it off, catching sight of the heavy black Bible sitting on the bedside table. It had been a long time since she'd felt the urge to read the Bible, a long time since she'd actually cared what God had to say to her. So many years of fighting for faith had left her with nothing but emptiness.

She lifted the Bible, carrying it from Sarah's room and into her own, opening to the page where births and deaths had been recorded for the past eighty years. John's name. Maddie's. Megan's.

She traced each one with her finger, then gently set the Bible down, lay on the bed, and prayed that sleep would take her.

TEN

Morning came way too soon. Jasmine groaned as the alarm clock rang, pulling the pillow over her head to block out the sound. She hadn't slept well at all. Dreams had chased her through the night and into the wee hours of the morning. She'd woken almost every hour, stared at the clock for what had seemed an eternity. Now she was paying for it, her head pounding, her eyes burning, her brain foggy.

She reached for the alarm, slamming her hand down on the snooze button and burrowing deeper into the covers. She'd stay here for a while. Maybe more than a while. Sarah wouldn't be back until after one. There was no sense getting up until just before that, because there was no way she was going to go to church feeling the way she did.

She'd almost convinced herself to stay put when the doorbell rang. She lifted her head, glanced at the clock. Eight. Whoever it was could go away and come back later. It rang again, this time more insistently, and Jasmine forced herself up and out of the room, tugging on a robe as she went.

"Who is it?"

"Eli."

"Eli?" She turned off the alarm, cracked open the door and peered out into gray morning light. "What are you doing here?"

"I was lonely. I thought you might be, too." He grinned, flashing straight white teeth.

"I'm not, so go away."

"Now that's not very neighborly. What would Sarah think?"

"She'd think you were rude for coming so early."

"Not if she knew I brought breakfast." He lifted a white paper bag speckled with oil stains.

"Breakfast?"

"Egg-and-cheese bagel for you. Sausage bagel for me."

"What if I want sausage?"

"You'll have to fight me for it."

"I'm not even dressed."

"So run and get dressed. I'll wait out here until you're done."

"Always the gentleman?"

"There's no other way to be."

It took Jazz five minutes to shower and dress. She figured she'd set a new world speed record, but Eli didn't look impressed as she opened the front door and let him in. "It's cold out here."

"You could have gone home."

"And missed having breakfast with a beautiful woman?"

"Sarah's not here. You'll have to settle for me."

"You really aren't good at taking compliments, are you?" He eyed her curiously as she set plates on the table and started a pot of coffee.

"My mother always said that men who made compliments a habit were about as trustworthy as a rabid raccoon."

"She had an interesting view of life."

"She had enough experience to know what she was talking about."

"Your father wasn't trustworthy?"

"My father was nonexistent. Mom gave me his name, but told me he wanted nothing to do with me. He even made her sign papers saying she wouldn't pursue any legal claim."

"Nice."

"Yeah. He was married. A high-powered attorney. The way Mom told it, he claimed he'd take custody of me if she didn't sign. She didn't think that would be such a healthy thing for her child, so she did what he asked."

"You ever look him up?"

"No. I've never even been tempted. The way I see it, I'm better off not knowing him." She poured coffee, handed a cup to him. "How about you? Are your father and mother together?"

"Joined at the hip. Except when Dad goes hunting or Mom goes antiquing. Then they separate for a while."

"Sounds nice."

"Yeah. It is. It's good to know couples can still stay together if they put their minds and hearts to it." He handed her a wrapped sandwich, then took a seat. "Better eat quick. Church starts in less than an hour."

"I'm staying home today."

"That seems a shame seeing as how you're dressed and ready to go."

"I'm wearing jeans and a T-shirt."

"God won't care what you're wearing. He'll just care that you're there."

"You may be right, but it's not Him I'm worried about. Sarah will be embarrassed if I show up at church like this."

"Who said Sarah has to see you? I was thinking we'd go to Fellowship Community Church together."

Surprised, she looked up from the bagel she was tearing apart. "What?"

"People will be a lot more likely to spill their guts to a pretty woman than to me."

Pretty and *stunning*. Did he really think that about her? Jasmine's cheeks heated and she looked down at the torn bagel. "Getting people to spill their guts isn't my thing."

"Just follow my lead and you'll be fine."

"I don't know, Eli."

"I do." He grabbed her hand, forcing her to stop the bagel mutilation. "We're both after the same goal. We want to find out what's going on. We can work alone, or we can work together. It seems to me, working together will save us time and effort."

Why couldn't he be spouting conspiracy theories and talking like a lunatic? That would make it easy to say no, to escort him to the door and send him on his way.

Instead, he was being completely rational, completely reasonable, completely impossible to ignore. "All right. I'll come with you, but I'm not wearing this. If Reverend McKenna is as old school as everyone says, he's not going to appreciate a woman showing up in jeans." She stood, tossing the remnants of breakfast into the trash and hurrying from the room.

Eli took a last sip of coffee, then rinsed out his cup and Jasmine's before placing them in the dishwasher. She hadn't eaten much. Not more than a quarter of the sandwich he'd brought. He shouldn't be noticing such things, or worrying that she was going to fade away to nothing if she didn't put some meat on her bones. Not that she didn't look fine just the way she was. She'd looked thin in her baggy, faded jeans and fitted T-shirt, but not skinny. Just right was more like it.

Which had absolutely nothing to do with his reasons for being in Lakeview, and he'd do well to remember that.

He scowled as he wiped a paper towel over the table and tossed it into the trash can. He'd thought about telling her to forget changing and concentrate on getting some food into her system, but he'd known she wouldn't listen. Besides, she'd been dead-on when she'd said Reverend McKenna wouldn't be happy about a woman showing up at his church in jeans.

His church. Not God's church. That was the impression Eli had gotten when he'd chanced a visit the previous day. McKenna didn't walk, he strutted like a well-fed peacock through the hallowed walls of God's house, his dark hair falling to his shoulders, his eyes feverishly bright as he'd explained the church's philosophy and purpose. Or maybe Eli's perception was skewed because of what he suspected.

"Ready." Jasmine walked into the room and all thoughts of McKenna fled Eli's head.

She'd changed, all right. No more faded jeans and fitted T-shirt, no more pale, makeup-free face and wildly curling hair. She'd put on a slim black skirt that reached her knees and a light purple sweater that hugged her slender curves. Schoolteacher modest, but on her... Well, on her it was enough to make a man want to take a second look. And a third. And a fourth.

"Wow."

"Thanks." She blushed, high heels clicking as she moved across the room and grabbed her purse. She'd put on makeup that deepened the color of her eyes and made them into mysterious pools that Eli was pretty sure he wouldn't mind exploring. A subtle citrusy perfume filled the air as she moved past. Delicate with just a hint of spice to it. A perfect match for the wearer.

"You're staring again."

"You're gorgeous."

"Eli—"

"You know what my gran always says?" He put a hand on her shoulder, warmth spearing through him as his fingers curved around tight muscle and delicate bone.

She shook her head, her barely tamed curls brushing against his knuckles, making him want to weave his fingers into her hair, feel the soft weight of it slide against his skin. "No. But I bet you're going to tell me."

"You're right. I am. Gran always says the best thing to do with a compliment is to tuck it away in your heart. That way when bad days come, which they always do, you can pull it out and hang on to it."

"She really says that?"

"She really does."

"I'd like to meet your gran one day." She smiled, her lips glossy and pink. Perfect for kissing. Which Eli had absolutely no intention of doing. Somehow, though, he was leaning closer, staring into her eyes, seeing something flare to life in the depth of her gaze, and feeling his heart quicken in response.

"And I know for a fact Gran would love to meet you." *Pull back, man. You kiss her now and you'll blow it for sure.* The thought whispered through his mind, and he decided it might be a good one to heed. Jasmine would run far and fast if he kissed her now. Besides, he hadn't come to Lakeview to get involved with a woman. He'd come to find Rebecca. Until he did that, he really shouldn't be gazing into a beautiful woman's eyes, or imagining what her lips would feel like against his.

She frowned, her eyes turning dark with whatever she was thinking. "You know, maybe it's better if I don't come to church with you."

"I thought we'd already decided that we'd accomplish more together than we would alone."

Sure they'd decided that. Before Jasmine had seen the look in Eli's eyes. She knew attraction when she saw it, and that's what she'd been seeing. That was what she'd been *feeling*.

She yanked open the front door and stepped outside, hoping the icy wind would slap some sense into her besotted head. No, not besotted. She was *not* anything close to that. She'd just been temporarily swayed by Eli's golden eyes, his easy smile, his gentle touch. Now she was better. Firmly in the moment, focused on the job of finding out if someone was after Sarah. "You're right. I'm just worried I'll say something that'll make people suspicious."

"You've got nothing to worry about. Besides, we can't close doors that God opens. He'll direct us to the people we need to speak to, and He'll give us the words we need to say."

"I'm glad you're so confident."

"What's not to be confident about? Worse case scenario, we go and we get nothing but an earful of the pompous pastor's preaching."

"Pompous pastor's preaching? You've got quite a way with words, Eli." Laughter bubbled up and spilled out as she spoke, Jasmine's heart feeling lighter than it had in a long time.

The thought sobered her. Was she forgetting her family so soon? Three years didn't seem nearly enough time to get used to life without her husband and children. A lifetime wouldn't be enough. And yet, she was laughing as if she didn't have a care in the world, enjoying Eli's company, letting him fill some of the emptiness.

She couldn't decide if that was good or bad. All she knew was that it was a change. The tide that had swept her away from life had turned and was dragging her back in whether she liked it or not.

Eli slid into his seat, turned on the car and smiled in her direction, his presence filling the car, filling her mind, driving away the sadness that had claimed it.

"Ready?"

"As I'll ever be."

"Then let's do it." He pulled down the driveway and onto the main thoroughfare, the house disappearing from view, the road beckoning Jasmine forward while little-girl giggles echoed through in her head, reminding her that forward couldn't offer her the one thing she wanted more than anything—more time with the family she'd loved so desperately. One more week. One more day. One more minute.

Eli shifted slightly, his hand wrapping around hers, squeezing gently, as if he sensed her thoughts and her sorrow. As if he could somehow absorb some of what she was feeling and make it easier to bear.

She knew she should pull away, refuse the contact and the comfort, but she didn't. Instead, she let the heat of his touch melt away the bitter chill of loss and chase away a small measure of the pain that lived in her heart.

For right now, that was enough.

ELEVEN

The church was deep in the foothills of the Blue Ridge Mountains, the winding road that led to it lined by tall trees that cast shadows and darkened the landscape. Despite the welcome sign and the open door, the place didn't look inviting and Jasmine felt a shiver of foreboding as she stepped out of Eli's SUV. "So this is it."

"Yep. This is it."

"I don't like it." She whispered the words as he came around the car and hooked an arm through hers.

"What's bothering you about it?" His eyes scanned her face, intent and questioning.

"Maybe just the fact that I know the pastor has lost two wives in the past five years. Maybe it just seems dark. Creepy even."

"Yeah?" He glanced around, his gaze seeming to take in everything—the half-full parking lot, the towering trees, the well-manicured grass. In the distance, a small white farmhouse sat on a hill, and he pointed to it. "The parsonage. The reverend has been living there since he took the position."

"How do you learn all these things?"

"I ask questions. People give me answers of one sort or another. Come on. Let's see if we can get a front pew."

A front pew? She was thinking more along the lines of something in the back. Maybe something outside the front door.

"Listen," he said, leaning close to her ear as they moved up the stairs toward the door. "We've got to pretend we're an item, let people think we're looking for a new church home. They'll be more likely to chat that way."

"All right. I've got no problem with that."

"Good, then you won't mind if I do this." He wrapped his arm around her waist and tugged her close. She could feel the warmth of his body from her shoulder to her hip, and knew her cheeks were the color of ripe tomatoes.

As they stepped into the sanctuary, several people turned in their pews, their eyes filled with speculation and curiosity. Maybe they didn't get guests very often and were wondering who Jasmine and Eli were. Then again, a lot of the people who were staring were women. They might be more interested in finding out whether or not Eli and Jasmine's relationship was serious than they were in getting to know the new couple.

"Welcome to Fellowship Community Church. Our doors are always open and we're so happy to see you've walked through them."

Jasmine turned her attention to the speaker—a tall thin man in his mid-to-late forties. An usher pin on his lapel stated his name—Brother Cornell. The name was familiar. Was this Mary's father? An uncle?

"I'm Brother Jackson Cornell. One of the elders here. If you'd fill out this visitor form, we'd truly appreciate it." He was speaking to Eli, nearly ignoring Jasmine's presence. She didn't care; she wasn't sure she'd want to be speared beneath his mud-brown gaze.

"Thank you, Mr. Cornell. I'm—"

"It's Brother Cornell. We are all part of the same family." He flashed a smile that did nothing to settle Jasmine's churning stomach.

"Brother Cornell, then. I'm Eli Jennings. I stopped by yesterday to speak with Reverend McKenna and decided to come in for the service. This is my friend, Jasmine."

"Nice to meet you both. I'm sure you'll enjoy the reverend's sermon. He knows the word of God, nearly breathes it out of his pores."

"Sounds like he's just the kind of guy who belongs in the pulpit." Eli continued speaking as they moved up the aisle toward the front of the church.

"No doubt about it. He's brought life back into this dead place."

"Dead?" Eli slid into the front pew and Jasmine had no choice but to follow.

"Seven years ago this church was near extinction. After nearly a century of serving the community, we were talking about closing the doors."

"And Reverend McKenna changed all that?"

"Yes, he did. He brought people and life back into Fellowship Community. He's a true godsend. Our membership is up to nearly a hundred and fifty from less than thirty."

"That's fantastic."

"Sure is. Now, I've got to go greet some others, so you just have a seat and fill out the card. Throw it in the collection plate. Service will start shortly." He hurried away, and Jasmine sank into the pew next to Eli, her heart hammering too fast.

Her faith might be raw and wounded, but she'd always found comfort in God's house. Not here, though. Here she felt a sense of unease that wouldn't leave as organ music began to play and the pews filled up behind her.

A tall, gaunt man with shoulder-length hair sauntered up to the pulpit, his dark eyes burning with a fire that made Jasmine shudder. This was Reverend McKenna? She'd imagined someone a little short, a little stout, maybe red-haired and angry-eyed. A tough, rough, outdoorsy type. Not a man who looked like an angst-ridden poet.

His eyes scanned the congregation, settling on her as he spoke. "We welcome all who come to worship our God and King. Please stand as we praise the Lord in song." He signaled the organist and led the congregation in a rather somber and slow version of a praise song popular when Jasmine was a kid.

"The song is cheerful enough to make you want to come back for more, isn't it?" Eli whispered in her ear, and Jasmine was sure the reverend heard. His eyes darkened, his thin mouth turned down as he shifted his attention from Jasmine to Eli.

"Shhhhh. The reverend is watching."

"And that should scare me because…?"

"He's creepy."

"I've seen a lot creepier."

Another song followed the first, just as slow and somber. After that, announcements were made and an offering was collected. Jasmine could feel the reverend's gaze as she dropped a few dollars into the plate. What was with him? Was he just curious? Did he sense that she and Eli were here because they thought he was lying about his wife's disappearance?

No. Of course he didn't. She was just reading into the situation because she was nervous.

"Relax, Jasmine. We're fine. Reverend McKenna can't hurt us."

Maybe not, but Jasmine didn't like him, and relaxing was

difficult when her heart was threatening to leap out of her chest. By the time the hour-long sermon on the importance of tithing was over, Jasmine was ready to go home. Forget asking questions, forget trying to find out what had happened to McKenna's first wife, she wanted out of the church and away from the strangely somber congregation.

Unfortunately, Eli had other plans. He held her hand and stood, preventing Jasmine from bolting as several parishioners approached.

"It's so good to see you here this morning." A petite woman with white hair and dark brown eyes smiled brightly as she offered her hand. "I'm Laura Cornell, Jackson's wife. I believe you met him before the service."

"We sure did, ma'am." Eli returned the woman's smile.

"Did you enjoy the sermon?"

"The reverend sure does have a way with scripture." Eli's answer was vague and noncommittal, but Laura didn't seem to notice.

She smiled, nodded. "Yes, he does. Are you two from this area?"

"We drove here from Lakeview."

"Then you traveled a bit of a distance to get here. We're having a barbecue at the reverend's house. Why don't you join us?"

"We couldn't impose like that." Jasmine hurried to speak, afraid Eli would accept. She felt spooked enough. She did not want to spend time with the reverend.

"Impose? How could it possibly be an imposition? We're all part of God's family. What we have, we gladly share." She'd seemed normal until now, but her voice had taken on an odd inflection as if she were reciting someone else's words and thoughts.

"That's very nice of you, Mrs. Cornell, but I do have to

get Jasmine back home. Her mother-in-law hasn't been well, and she needs to be there to take care of her."

"Oh, I'm so sorry to hear that."

"Thank you." Jasmine squeezed Eli's hand, hoping he'd get the idea and start moving the conversation along so they could make their escape.

"Is your husband there with her now?"

"Excuse me?" Jazz wasn't sure she'd heard right. It had been a long time since anyone had asked her about her husband.

"Is your husband at home with your mother-in-law?" Laura repeated the question, her dark gaze steady and disconcerting.

"No, she's with a friend. My husband passed away three years ago."

"I'm so sorry. I know what it's like to lose family. My parents have been gone for years. You never stop missing them, do you?"

"No. You don't."

"Laura. It's time to leave." Jackson strode up beside his wife, his expression guarded as he glanced from Eli to Jasmine.

"I was just thinking that we should invite Jasmine and Eli to our Wednesday-night potluck."

"That sounds like a wonderful way to get to know our new friends." The voice came from behind Jasmine, soft and gentle, but somehow chilling.

She turned to face Reverend McKenna, bracing herself for his intense stare, but he was looking at Eli, a smile curving his thin lips. "Eli, it's good to see you again."

"Good to see you, too, Reverend."

"Have you had any success locating Rebecca?"

"I'm afraid not."

"If you do, please tell her that I forgive her for the wrong she's done me."

"I will."

"And let her brother know that I did the best I could to make her happy."

"Of course."

"Thank you." He shifted his gaze to Jasmine. "You're Sarah's daughter-in-law."

How did he know? She didn't dare ask, so she nodded instead. "That's right."

"I heard she had an accident recently."

"She fell down a flight of stairs."

"I'm sorry to hear that. Is there anything our church can do to help?"

"I think she's doing okay now, but thank you for offering." Her skin felt clammy, her heart racing.

"It's the least we can do. Sarah has been an inspiration to so many—building a business while raising a child, then offering job opportunities to young people in the community. Truly an inspiration."

"I'll tell her you said so."

"Please do." He flashed teeth that looked too white for his worn and faded face. "You will join us on Wednesday, won't you?"

"Oh, I don't think—"

"We'd be happy to." Eli cut her off before she could refuse the offer, and Jasmine shot him a look.

"Eli will be, but I've got to stay with Sarah. She's still not herself."

"I understand. Perhaps another time." Reverend McKenna smiled again. "If you'll excuse me. I've got many other brothers and sisters to visit with today."

Jasmine breathed a sigh of relief as he walked away,

hoping she and Eli could finally start moving toward the door. Maybe a subtle hint was in order. "We'd better go, too."

"Your mother-in-law is Sarah Hart?" Laura put a hand on Jasmine's arm, holding her in place.

"Yes."

"Please tell her that my husband and I are desperate to see our daughter again. She'll know who I'm talking about."

"I—"

"Please. Mary is my only daughter. I won't go see her if she doesn't want me to, but I need to know she's okay." There were tears in Laura's eyes, and Jasmine patted her hand, knowing the depth of despair she was feeling, the horrible emptiness of loss.

"I'll tell her."

"No need to tell her anything. We'll find our daughter on our own."

"Jackson!"

"Sarah Hart turned our daughter against us. I want nothing else from that woman, or anyone associated with her."

Shocked, Jasmine tried to reason with the man. "I'm sure Sarah didn't mean to hurt your family in any way."

"Didn't mean to? She did everything she could to undermine my authority with my daughter. If I had my way she'd be in jail for corrupting a minor. As a matter of fact—"

"Isn't your daughter eighteen?" Eli's question cut Jackson's tirade short.

"My daughter's age has nothing to do with it. She was young and impressionable and Sarah Hart stole her away from us. Let's go, Laura." He turned abruptly and strode off, his stiff movements filled with anger.

"Please. Tell Sarah." Laura whispered the plea as she followed her husband out of the church.

"Well, that was interesting." Eli grabbed Jasmine's hand and led her toward the exit.

"Disturbing is more like it." Jasmine shuddered as she remembered the anger in Jackson's eyes.

"Jackson definitely has something against Sarah."

"We should tell the sheriff."

"I agree. He can ask around and find out if Cornell was at the museum's grand opening." Eli opened the door to his SUV and Jasmine climbed in, remembering Laura's desperation and wondering what lengths she'd go to if one of her daughters was out in the world, alive but unreachable.

"You're deep in thought." Eli slid into the car and started the engine.

"I'm going to have to talk to Sarah again."

"About Mary?"

"I think she knows something, and I don't think it's right that she's keeping it from Mary's family."

"She may have a good reason."

"Then I hope she explains it to me. No mother should be kept away from her children." She sounded a lot more vehement than she'd meant to, so she cleared her throat and tried again. "Laura seems like a really nice lady. I hate to think that she's suffering when there's something I can do to help."

"Do you think Sarah will change her mind about sharing what she knows?"

"I think I've got to try and get her to."

Eli nodded, but didn't speak again as he drove back toward Lakeview.

Jasmine let the silence fill her, let her mind wonder in the solitude it created. To have a daughter out in the world and not know where she was seemed the worst kind of punishment. If her daughters were alive, she'd go to any means necessary to find them. No matter what, she'd make sure she had a chance to tell them again how much she loved them. If she could, she'd give Laura that opportunity. Even if that meant another argument with Sarah.

TWELVE

Sarah arrived home from church well rested and cheerful. Jasmine hated to ruin her mood, but she was anxious to get the discussion about Mary out of the way.

"You look tired, dear. Didn't you sleep well?" Sarah lowered herself into a kitchen chair and grabbed the paperback lying on the table.

"Not really. I had a lot on my mind."

"Like what?"

"The two missing women—Rebecca and Mary."

"You shouldn't concern yourself with them, dear. I'm sure they're both fine."

"I'm not. And neither is Mary's mother."

"You spoke to Laura Cornell?"

"Eli and I went to Fellowship Community Church to see what we could find out about Reverend McKenna's wives."

"Did you learn anything?"

"I learned that Laura is desperate for information about her daughter."

"And?"

"I think you may know where she is."

"I'm afraid I've got nothing to say on the subject."

"Sarah—"

"I gave Mary my word. I can't break it."

"Her mother is distraught. Can you imagine how hard it must be to know your daughter is out there somewhere and you're unable to find her?"

"No, because I can't imagine ever doing something that would send my daughter running."

"You're being unreasonable."

"So are you. You know nothing about the situation, and, quite honestly, you know nothing about me. If I hadn't broken my hip, you'd still be living your life in New Hampshire, doing everything you could to avoid my calls."

"I never avoided your calls!" But, of course, she had. Hearing Sarah's voice on her answering machine had evoked emotions Jasmine had been trying hard to push to the back of her mind and her life. She'd wanted to forget, not remember.

"Of course you avoided me. Did you think I wouldn't notice that you only called on Sundays when you knew I would be at church?"

"I—" She stopped before she could protest. That was exactly what she'd done. "Look, Sarah, I didn't mean to hurt you. I just needed some time to heal."

"So did I. And I needed my family with me while I did it. Or maybe it never occurred to you that that's what we are." She got up way too quickly, shrugging off Jasmine's help as she moved into her bedroom.

"Sarah—"

"I've said all I have to say on the subject." Sarah closed the door, the quiet click ending the conversation.

Maybe it was for the best. Jasmine had no excuse for what she'd done. Grief had made her into the kind of person she'd never thought she would be.

The doorbell rang and she hurried to answer it, glad for

the distraction. Eli stood outside, his eyes blazing gold in a deeply tan face, a soft smile playing on his lips. Maybe she'd been expecting to see him, because Jasmine wasn't surprised by his presence. Instead, she was warmed by it, happiness curling around her heart and squeezing hard. "Eli. Hi."

"Hi, yourself." He scanned her face, frowned. "What's wrong? You look like you lost your best friend."

"Just Sarah's affection."

"I doubt that." He put a hand on her shoulder, urging her deeper into the room so he could shut the door. "Sarah doesn't seem the kind to withdraw affection very easily."

"Who said it was easy? I've pretty much avoided her for the past three years."

"You lost your husband and children, and you needed time to recover from that."

"That's what I told myself, but I think I was just taking the easy way out." She tried to smile, but failed.

"You can't beat yourself up because your way of grieving is different from Sarah's."

"Can't I?" She settled down onto the couch, expecting that Eli would take a seat in the easy chair as he'd done before. Instead, he sat beside her. Close enough that she could feel his warmth and smell the clean scent of his shampoo.

"No. You can't. Guilt is useless. It only makes life more difficult."

"You sound like you know what you're talking about."

"I do." His eyes were dark with sadness, and Jazz reached for his arm, wrapping her fingers around firm muscle.

"What do you feel guilty about?"

"Living." His lips quirked in a half smile that only partly took the darkness from his gaze. "I lost five buddies in one day. I was a couple of pints of blood away from dying myself. It's easy to ask why I was spared and they weren't."

"God has His reasons." She'd heard the platitude a million times and offered it now by rote.

"He does, but that doesn't make it any easier to bear, now does it?"

"No, it doesn't."

"The way I see it, I can waste time feeling guilty, or I can spend it honoring the lives of those who died."

"That's why you write what you do?"

"I never thought about it that way, but maybe." He smiled, staring into Jasmine's eyes, connecting with a part of her that should have died with John and the girls, but which suddenly seemed very much alive.

She started to move away, but Eli's hand slid over hers, covering her knuckles and pressing her palm more firmly against his arm. "Don't be scared of what you're feeling, Jasmine."

"I don't know what you're talking about." But she did. Her heart pounded in her chest, as Eli leaned closer, his gaze drifting from her eyes to her lips and settling there.

Move! Now!

But she was frozen in place, unable to move and not even sure she wanted to.

"Eli! I thought I heard voices out here." Sarah shuffled into the room, her words like a splash of ice water in Jasmine's face.

Jazz jumped back, hurrying to her feet and watching as Eli stood and offered Sarah a hand, helping as she lowered herself onto the couch. "It's good to see you, Sarah. Did you have fun with Mrs. Walker?"

"The woman is a menace. She invited half the church over for breakfast this morning. We were crowded into her house like sardines. But it *was* fun."

Funny, when Jasmine had asked the same question, she'd gotten a three-word answer—*it was fine.*

"As long as it was fun and you made it back home in one piece, I guess being a sardine for a while isn't so bad." Eli settled into the easy chair, and it seemed as though he planned to stay there for a while, his long legs stretched out in front of him, his expression relaxed and open. It was hard to believe he carried guilt and grief inside.

"True. I was due for a little fun after a week and a half in the hospital and a week trapped in the house. Of course, since Jasmine arrived, things have been much better." She shot Jasmine a small smile by way of apology, and Jasmine smiled back. It would take time to rebuild what they'd had before John and the girls had been taken from them, but it would happen. Jasmine refused to believe anything else.

Sarah turned her attention back to Eli. "Did you stop by for a reason, or just to visit, Eli?"

"A little of both. Jasmine and I have plans for Wednesday night, I wanted to confirm them. I also wanted to make sure you were okay."

"Plans?"

"We're going to a potluck together."

"No, we're not." Jasmine sputtered the protest, but neither Eli nor her mother-in-law paid any attention.

"That sounds like fun, and since you'll both be gone that night, I think I'll have Germaine take me to church. We've got prayer meeting."

"Sounds good. Just stay alert and be careful."

"No need to worry about that, young man. I've got no intention of giving my attacker a second chance to do me in."

Eli's lips twitched, his eyes warm with humor. "Good to hear. I guess everything went well last night. No problems?"

"Problems? No. But Germaine was sure we were being followed on the way to her house."

"What!" Jasmine straightened. "You didn't tell me that."

"Because we weren't being followed. You know how vivid Germaine's imagination is."

"Still, you should have called the police and let them know."

"Let them think I'm paranoid? No thanks. I'll save my calls for times when I really need help." Sarah dug into the pocket of her slacks, pulling out a piece of paper and turning her attention back to Eli. "I've got something for you, Eli, but you've got to promise not to give it to anyone else."

"You've got my word on that, Sarah."

"Good. This is Mary's address and phone number. I helped her get a job with an old friend of mine in West Virginia. Mary is working while she attends community college there. After thinking and praying about it, I realized it wouldn't be right for me to withhold information that might help you locate Rebecca."

Eli took the piece of paper. "This means a lot to me, Sarah. And it'll mean a lot to my friend Marcus."

"Tell him it's my way of thanking him for his service."

"I'll do that."

"And, please, don't even pass Mary's whereabouts on to him. There are issues I'm not at liberty to discuss, but suffice to say that Mary is very determined to stay hidden."

"I wouldn't betray your trust like that."

"I'm sure you wouldn't." Sarah shot Jasmine with a look that made her cheeks heat.

"I wouldn't either, Sarah."

"I hope not."

The comment stung, though Jasmine was sure Sarah hadn't intended it to. She stood, smiling, trying to act as if she weren't hurt. "I hope you two will excuse me, but I've got some work that needs to be done."

She hurried down the hall before either could try to stop her. Not that either did. No one called for her to return. No one asked her to stay. Jasmine was surprised at how much it bothered her. She'd thought she was content to move through the world alone; that she'd gotten used to the solitary life she'd created. Maybe she'd been wrong.

She grabbed her sketch pad, then finished up the last sketch for the alphabet book with the quick ease that came from practice. She'd drawn a dozen or more prancing zebras in the past few years. Sometimes they'd had a vague resemblance to Danielle Donkey. This one did, the large deep eyes, the faintly smiling mouth. It would be so easy to write another Danielle book. Her editor had asked over and over again, but Jasmine had declined. She'd written the series for her girls. Without them, there was no reason to continue.

A soft tap sounded at the window, and Jasmine jumped, dropping the sketch pad onto the bed, her heart slamming in her chest. Another tap, and she crossed the room, pulling up the shade, expecting to see... She wasn't sure what she expected to see. Certainly not Eli, standing outside in the gray afternoon light.

She opened the window and the screen, telling herself she wasn't happy to see him and knowing she was lying. "What are you doing out there?"

"Enjoying the scenery." He grinned, grabbing her hand and tugging gently. "Come on out."

"I'm too old to sneak out windows."

"Who said anything about sneaking?" Before she knew what he was doing, he put both hands under her arms and lifted her, pulling her out through the window and setting her on her feet.

It was cold, but her cheeks were flaming, her heart tap dancing to the tune of her racing pulse. "You're lucky you didn't break your back."

"Lifting you?" He laughed, grabbing her hand and leading her down toward the lake. "It would take five of you to do that."

"If you're going to try to convince me to go with you Wednesday night, forget it."

"The thought had crossed my mind."

"It's not like we got any information today. Going to Fellowship Community was a waste of time."

"I wouldn't call it that. We learned Mary's parents are worried, that her father is angry with Sarah, and that her mother is desperate to find her."

"We also know the reverend is creepy."

"That, too." As he spoke, he unzipped his coat and settled it around her shoulders, enveloping her in leather and the strong masculine scent that was uniquely Eli's.

She wanted to burrow deep into the folds of the coat, accept the warmth and the companionship Eli wanted to offer, but her mind jumped back in time—walking along this same path with John, his coat zipped up to her chin, his arm heavy around her shoulder—and her throat closed tight with tears she would not shed.

"I need to go back to the house. If Sarah realizes I'm missing she'll be worried." Her words were thick with unshed tears, but if Eli noticed he didn't let on.

"No she won't. She gave me permission to steal you away for a while."

"You actually told her you were going to drag me out the window?"

"Sure did. My gran always says it's best to be clear about your intentions. Saves a lot of explaining later on."

Intentions? What kind of intentions was he talking about? Jasmine didn't know, and she wasn't sure she wanted to. Not now anyway. Not when it was so easy to walk with Eli, to talk to him, share with him. She'd missed that easy companionship more than she'd wanted to acknowledge.

"Sarah's a good lady. She didn't mean to hurt you." His

words were quiet, barely intruding on her thoughts, and for a moment Jasmine considered ignoring them. One thing she'd learned growing up, though, ignoring things didn't make them go away. Pretending she and Sarah didn't have issues wouldn't help solve the trouble that was between them. And despite the years that had passed, Jasmine still loved her mother-in-law.

"I know that."

"Then why are you so sad?" He stopped, turning so that they were face-to-face, his broad shoulders blocking her view of the lake, his eyes gentle.

"Because *I* hurt *her*. Everything was so hard after John and the girls died. I just wanted to forget, but I couldn't, and talking to Sarah made the memories that much more vivid. Her voice, her inflections, the way she saw the world, they were John all over again."

"I'm sure she understood."

"How could she? We were family. Then we weren't. Not because of her, but because of me."

"You will be again. Just give it some time."

"Time isn't our friend, Eli. One minute you're holding someone you love. The next they're out of your reach. I don't want to have that happen before Sarah and I make amends."

"So tell her that."

"It's not that easy."

"It's as easy as you allow it to be." He squeezed her hand. "You said it yourself, Jasmine. There are no guarantees in life. We have exactly this moment. How can any of us allow hard feelings to fester if we really understand that?"

He was right. Of course he was. She sighed, pulling off his coat and handing it back to him. "I guess it's time that Sarah and I had a talk."

"Want me to come?"

"No. But thanks for offering and for…everything."

She walked back to the house, sensing Eli's gaze, but not acknowledging it as she clambered back into the window and went to talk to Sarah.

THIRTEEN

Wednesday morning dawned like every other one had in the past few days. Cold and gray. Eli grimaced as he pulled back the curtains in the living room and stared toward the green-blue lake. It was a little past seven, the sky still more dark than light, but if he was going to run, now was the time to do it. Otherwise, he'd wimp out and stay in where it was warm. He could just hear Marcus howling with laughter if he learned that Eli had opted to stay inside rather than go for his morning run. And knowing Marcus, he *would* find out. The guy had eyes and ears everywhere. Too bad they hadn't been effective when it came to finding Rebecca.

As if on cue, Eli's cell phone rang. He answered as he stepped out into the brisk morning air. "Jennings, here. What's up?"

"Me. That's what. And I'm not happy about it, but it was the only time I could get a call through. Hear anything?" Marcus's voice grumbled in his ear, and Eli wished he had more to tell him.

"Just the same story you were told. Rebecca met a man at college, fell in love, ran away with him. I did find out some interesting information about McKenna's first wife."

"Yeah?"

"Her illness was never diagnosed. The coroner's report said she died of heart failure, but her body had been attacked by something for a long time before that."

"You go to the sheriff with that?"

"Yes, but it didn't do me much good. He didn't see the connection. I'm still looking, though. Two mysteries in one man's life seem like an awful lot."

"No other leads?"

"One. A teenage girl who disappeared a couple of days after Rebecca. She was a member of McKenna's church and, from what I've heard, good friends with Rebecca."

"You know where she is?"

"I've got contact information, but either she's moved or she's not answering her phone."

"Go find out. I'll pay for the trip."

"You're not paying for anything. We're friends, man." Eli started jogging, taking the sloping path down toward the lake, then veering sharply toward the ranch house. Just a quick peek to make sure both ladies were still tucked safely away in the house. That was what he told himself, though the truth was probably a lot less altruistic.

"When are you going to pay her a visit?"

"Tomorrow. Tonight I'm heading back to Fellowship Community Church."

"You don't think that's a dead end?"

"I think someone there knows more than he's saying. I'm willing to do what it takes to find out what that is."

"Just don't get arrested. No way can I get back there to bail you out."

"You just get back here in one piece. That's all I'm worried about."

"Three months and I'll be Stateside. Hopefully, I'll know more about Rebecca by then."

"I'm going to keep digging until I have the answers you need."

"Yeah, but they won't be the answers I want. Rebecca's not going to suddenly appear, healthy and happy." And alive. The last words were unspoken, but ringing loudly in Eli's ears.

"You don't know that for sure, Marcus."

"If my sister were alive, she'd have contacted me by now. What I need is justice and closure."

"Like I said, I'll keep digging."

"Thanks, buddy. I've got to take off. I need sleep to keep my head on straight in this mess."

"Watch your back."

"You, too."

Eli shoved the phone into the pocket of his jacket, worried about his friend and frustrated with how little he'd learned about Rebecca's life. She hadn't been a young bride—a few years over thirty when she'd married. A teacher pursuing her master's degree, she'd met McKenna at a Christian single's retreat. By all accounts it had been love at first sight. Whether or not that love had lasted through the honeymoon and first and only year of their marriage was up for debate. What Eli had gleaned from the various opinions he'd collected was that eleven months wasn't a long time to be married, but it was long enough to see someone's true colors. There'd been tension between the reverend and his wife in the month before she'd disappeared, and neither had seemed particularly happy about the marriage.

Had Rebecca realized what she'd gotten herself into and flown the coop? Or had McKenna realized Rebecca couldn't be controlled and decided to get rid of her? Or was something else going on? Something Eli hadn't even thought of?

He quickened his pace as he rounded the corner of the

Harts' house. The doors and the windows of the rancher were closed, the shades drawn, everything quiet and sleepy. Just as it should be.

Both women were probably still asleep, though he found it hard to imagine Jasmine lying in bed for much longer than it took her to wake up in the morning. She wasn't a restful person. Energy hummed off her, crackling through the air and drawing his attention again and again whenever he was near her.

"Isn't it a little cold for an early morning run?" Jasmine called out from the old dock that jutted into the lake. Seeing her there made his heart skip a beat. The wood was old, half-rotted and not safe in his opinion.

"Better come off there before it gives out."

"I've got a guy coming out later to start working on it. I just wanted to make sure it wasn't going to collapse when he stepped out on it." That was what she said, but there was something in her hand—a long piece of wood that she held gingerly in her gloved fist.

"Is that why you're out so early?" He slowed to a brisk walk as he neared the lake.

Jasmine met him near the shore, her bright knit hat almost garish compared to the paleness of her face. "Partly."

"And the other part?"

"Too many pictures of my husband and children inside the house."

"I'm sorry." He told himself he shouldn't do it, but he took her hand anyway, leading her away from the lake and the rickety dock, back to the house she seemed to be constantly running from. "What were they like? Your family, I mean."

She stiffened at the question, and he was sure she wouldn't answer. Then she spoke quietly as if her memories were ones she didn't share often. "My husband was an accountant.

Smart. Funny. One of those steady kind of guys every parent wants their daughter to meet."

"Your mom liked him?"

"She'd passed away the summer before we met. I was eighteen and just starting college in Boston. A friend thought I needed a getaway and invited me down here for a week."

"And the rest is history."

"Yes. We married less than a year later. The girls were born five years after that. We'd wanted children so badly. They were our miracles." She smiled, the expression so sad it speared into Eli's heart.

"They were beautiful girls."

"Yes, but very different from each other. Meg was outgoing and spunky. Maddie was our dreamer. I often thought she'd be a writer or an artist one day. Of course, that wasn't meant to be. Sometimes, if I'm really quiet, I'm sure I can hear their laughter still echoing in the air." She hadn't pulled her hand from his, and Eli tugged her closer, letting his arm slip around her waist, anchoring her to his side.

"Memories are powerful things."

"Yes, they are. Do you think about your friends often? The ones you lost in Iraq?"

"Maybe not consciously, but they're always in my mind." Always impacting the choices he made, the places he went. God had given him a second chance at life. Knowing how many of his buddies had died only made that seem more precious.

"That's how it feels, isn't it? As if they're always just on the other side of your thoughts?"

"Exactly."

"The problem is, when I'm here they're everywhere I look. Every tree, every blade of grass, every place we walked and talked. Even here." She turned over the piece of wood she was holding, and Eli could see the names carved into it. John, Jasmine, Megan, Maddie.

Jasmine freed her hand from his, running a finger over the worn letters and softened wood. "I remember the day we carved this. It was Megan's idea. Just the kind of thing she loved to do. Make a statement. Let people know she was there." She sniffed, but her eyes were dry.

"It must be incredibly hard to go on without them."

"Thanks for saying that." She placed the piece of wood beneath an azalea bush that abutted the side of the house, sheltering it under the bare branches.

When she spoke again, it was to change the subject, her face set into a forced smile. "Where were you jogging to?"

"Somewhere warmer than this." He kept his tone light, hooking his arm around her waist and tugging her a few steps away from the azalea and the carved plank.

"That's right. I forgot that your thin Southern blood can't take the cold."

"I believe you called me *wimpy*."

"Well, I'm not the one shivering."

"Shivering. I'm surprised we're not both blocks of ice by now."

"Come inside and have some coffee. That'll warm you up." She moved toward the back door of the house, and Eli allowed himself to be pulled along with her. Skipping a morning run because it was too cold was one thing. Skipping it because a gorgeous woman invited him in for coffee was something else entirely.

The house was somber in its silence, the brightly painted kitchen somehow faded and worn. "Is Sarah up?"

"If she is, she's hiding out in her room."

"I guess there's a reason for that?"

"She isn't happy with me right now."

"I thought you were going to talk to her."

"I did. She didn't like what I had to say." Jasmine grabbed the carafe from the coffeemaker and poured two mugs, anxiety thrumming through her. She and Sarah had talked for all of fifteen minutes before she'd decided to admit that she'd paid off Lakeview Retreat's mortgage. To say that Sarah was upset was putting it mildly.

"Give her time, Jasmine."

"I am. Right now, though, I think she'd be happy if I high-tailed it back to New Hampshire and left her alone."

"I doubt it." His fingers brushed hers as he took the coffee she offered, his craggy, handsome face filled with compassion.

It seemed strange to be standing in the kitchen with him. Sharing coffee on a cold winter morning was something she'd only ever done with John. She wasn't quite sure how she felt about having the same experience with Eli. It was different, that was for sure. John had been analytical and slow to speak. Eli had ready answers and quick responses. John had been bookish and more likely to observe a race than to run one. Eli was hands-on with everything. Two very different men. And somehow they both seemed to fit her.

The thought made her cheeks heat, her pulse accelerate. Things were changing. As much as she might want to hold on to the past, she couldn't. That left her no choice but to move into the future. She just wasn't sure she knew how to do it.

"Hey, it's not that bad is it?" Eli took the coffee cup she'd been holding and set it on the counter, placing his own next to it, then settling his hands on her shoulders and staring down into her face. Reading her expression, seeming to see much more than other people did. Maybe even more than John had.

Guilt speared through her at the thought, and she lowered her gaze. "No, it's not. It's just a lot harder than I thought it would be." That was the truth, and as much of it as she was willing to give him.

"Life can be like that sometimes."

"Yeah. The problem is I've made my own trouble this time. I decided to pay off Sarah's mortgage. Without consulting her."

"I'm thinking Sarah isn't the kind to be happy about that."

"No, but it seemed like a good idea at the time. The bank was going to foreclose. Some guy called to ask if I'd convince Sarah to sell. I just thought it would be easier to do it and then tell her."

"It's not an unforgivable offense, Jasmine."

"Maybe not, but Sarah is a proud woman and she's definitely not happy with me right now."

"Like I said, give her time. She'll realize intentions are what count and that your intentions were good ones."

"We'll see. Right now, she's determined to spend the day and night with Germaine. She called her friend last night and insisted she come pick her up at noon for lunch, take her to church tonight, and let her stay over. She said it was because she'd had so much fun Saturday night. *I* say she wants to keep as far away from me as possible."

"She's got a bee in her bonnet. It'll buzz out eventually." He tugged her forward, wrapped her in strong arms and warmth.

She wanted to lean into him and allow herself to accept what she hadn't felt in far too long—the comfort of a man's touch, the strength that came from sharing a burden and allowing someone else to help carry it. He smoothed a hand over her hair, his palm settling at her nape, his thumb caressing the sensitive flesh behind her ear, and she wrapped her arms around his waist, leaning her head against his chest and listening to the soft thud of his heart. Taller, broader, firmer than John, but somehow Eli made her feel as if she'd found her way back home again.

Tears clogged her throat and filled her eyes, but she forced them away. No matter how it felt, it was only for a moment. She cleared her throat, let her arms drop from his sides and stepped away. "The good news is, I've decided I don't want to spend the entire evening in the house alone. I'm going to go to Fellowship Community with you."

"You don't have to do that, Jasmine. I'll come here after I'm done. Stay for a few hours so you won't be alone."

"I know I don't have to. I want to. Before Sarah decided I was the worst daughter-in-law imaginable, she told me that Mary seemed scared when she came to her for help. That's why Sarah is so determined to keep her whereabouts quiet."

"Scared, huh? Maybe that explains why she won't answer her phone."

"You've tried to contact her?"

"More than once. I'll be driving to West Virginia tomorrow to see if I can track her down at the address Sarah gave me."

"I hope you can. For your friend's sake."

"And for Sarah's."

"That, too, but since there haven't been any new incidents in the past few days, I'm hoping whatever has been happening to Sarah is over."

"Don't count on it. People don't just give up on vendettas. If that's what this is, then Sarah needs to stay on guard."

His words left Jasmine cold, and she grabbed her coffee, taking a quick sip of the lukewarm brew. "I'll tell her to be careful."

"And I'll see you tonight. Right now, I've got to finish my run." His easy smile melted her heart, and Jasmine felt something inside coming to life again. Maybe it was just fatigue playing tricks on her mind. Or maybe, just maybe, it was hope.

FOURTEEN

Sarah managed to stay in her room until Germaine arrived at a few minutes past twelve. Both women seemed determined to ignore Jasmine as they grabbed Sarah's overnight case and made their way out the front door.

Unfortunately, Jasmine was just as determined to be acknowledged. Eli had been right when he'd said someone with a vendetta wouldn't give up. If Jackson Cornell was trying to get revenge for what he thought Sarah had done to his family, he'd keep trying until he accomplished his goal. "You two be careful, okay?"

"We're adults, Jasmine. We're perfectly capable of taking care of ourselves without dire warnings from you." Germaine huffed the words. Obviously, she'd been informed of Jasmine's crimes.

"I know you are, but Eli said that Sarah is still in danger and you both need to be on the alert."

As she'd hoped, the mention of Eli's name gave both women pause.

Sarah looked directly at her for the first time all day. "It's sweet of him to be concerned. We'll be careful."

"I guess I'll see you tomorrow morning."

Sarah nodded and slid into Germaine's car before Jasmine

could do what she wanted and beg forgiveness. That was for the best. She'd already apologized more than once. Any more seemed like overkill. Eventually, Sarah would be ready to talk. Until then, Jasmine would just have to deal with her silence.

"It's my fault, Lord. I know that. I should have prayed about it. But it just doesn't seem like You answer. At least not in a way I can hear." She muttered the prayer as she went back into the house.

The quiet was dismal, and Jasmine crossed the room, picking up one of the photographs of her family. John, Maddie, Megan, Jasmine. All smiling at the camera, the deep blue lake glittering in the sunlight behind them. She remembered the moment. Fourth of July. Just six months before the accident. Life had seemed so definite then, so sure and steady. She'd imagined years stretching out in front of them, imagined growing old, watching her grandkids play at her feet. Anything had been possible.

It still is.

The thought whispered through her mind, disconcerting. Even upsetting. How could anything be possible when she'd lost everything? Then again, how could it not? Despite her floundering faith, she'd once believed that impossibilities could become reality. That was why she'd pursued her childhood dream of writing and illustrating children's fiction, and it was why she'd let herself believe that John really could commit to her for a lifetime. Sure, her mother had been abandoned by every man she'd ever loved, but Jasmine had truly believed her love for John was different, that the two of them could make a forever together.

And they had. Almost.

She sighed, setting the photo back on the shelf and getting to work straightening the living room. Karen would be in the following day to do her twice-weekly cleaning, but Jasmine needed something to do that didn't include dwelling on things she couldn't change. The more she straightened, though, the more photographs she discovered. Honeymoon and wedding photos. Baby photos of the girls. The trip to Disneyland. Hiking in the Blue Ridge Mountains. Horseback riding in Arizona. They'd fit a lot into the years they'd had. She supposed that was something to be thankful for.

A stack of paperback books in hand, she shoved open the door to Sarah's room and stepped inside. The curtains were drawn tight over the window, the musty medicinal smell of the room making Jasmine's stomach twist. She pulled open the curtains, cracked open the window, letting light and fresh air into the stuffy interior. Cups littered the bedside table, and Jasmine collected them, pausing when she spotted the Bible lying open on Sarah's bed, a photograph sitting next to it.

Jazz hadn't seen this one before, and she picked it up, her hands trembling as she realized what it was. John and the girls on New Year's Eve, goofy party hats on their heads, holding a sign the girls must have crafted with glue sticks and glitter. We Love You, Mom. Happy New Year!

If only she'd been there with them. Maybe they would have stayed an extra day. A few extra minutes. Just enough time to avoid the drunk driver who'd killed them.

If only.

Tears dripped onto the photo, and she brushed them off, her fingers tracing each face, her heart pounding a slow, terrible beat as she replaced the photo and lifted the Bible. Verses were highlighted in yellow. The theme—forgiveness. But Jazz couldn't forgive. Not herself, not the driver who'd had way too much to drink and not God. She let the Bible drop down onto Sarah's comforter and threw herself down beside it, thick, hot tears coursing down her face, wetting the comforter and her hair, the pungent scent of grief mixing with the stuffy air of the sickroom until she thought she'd suffocate.

It might have been minutes or hours later that the doorbell rang, dragging Jazz from the half sleep she'd fallen into. Tears hadn't made her feel better. Instead, she felt groggy.

The doorbell rang again and she forced herself off Sarah's bed and across the room. "I'm coming. Hold on."

She yanked the front door open, stepping aside as Eli moved into the room. "Is it time to go already?"

"I thought we'd drive to the store and get something to bring to the potluck before we went, but I'm thinking I should have called to let you know about the change in plans."

"It would have helped." She smiled, hoping the expression would wipe away whatever tears were still evident on her face. "I'll freshen up. Then we can go."

She started to walk away, but he grabbed her hand, pulling her to a stop. "You've been crying."

"And?"

"And I'm thinking maybe you're not up to going with me tonight."

"My other choice is to sit around here dwelling on a million regrets. I think I'd rather go." To her horror, more tears filled her eyes.

"A *million* regrets?" He tugged her close, pressing her head to his chest and stroking her hair.

"One big one."

"That you weren't with them when they died?"

She stilled at his words. "How did you know?"

"I'd feel the same if I were you."

"I should have been with them. I was *supposed* to be with them. I canceled at the last minute because I had a deadline looming."

"Things happen for a reason, Jasmine. And we're not always in control of them."

"I could have—"

"If you'd known, you *would* have, but you didn't know. You're a human being with a finite view of the world."

"I just wish…"

"What?" He wiped a tear from her cheek, his finger rough against her skin, his gaze filled with compassion. A soldier, a writer, a good friend. All those things, but who was Eli really, and what did he want from her besides help in finding Rebecca McKenna?

Maybe more importantly—what did *she* want from *him?* Nothing?

Everything?

The fact that she was even asking the questions worried her, and she turned away, hurried down the hall, calling over her shoulder as she went, "Help yourself to some coffee while I get ready."

By the time she'd reapplied her makeup, she'd composed herself enough to face Eli again. At least that was what she thought until she stepped into the living room and saw him stretched out in the easy chair. Her heart skipped, her pulse jumped and her mouth went dry. Like a kid with a crush. Worse. A grown woman with a crush.

The thought made her wince, and she grabbed her purse, ready to get out of the house and hopefully refocus her thinking. "Sorry for taking so long."

"That was long? My sisters used to take entire afternoons getting ready to go out. They probably still do."

"I always wondered what it would be like to have a sister."

"Well, I'll tell you. It was interesting. Nice in its own way. Though, I'd be lying if I said I didn't sometimes wish they were all boys. Course, I'm sure they often wished I was a girl.

Especially when they found wriggling critters in their patent-leather shoes."

"You didn't."

"I did." He grinned, his hand warm at the small of Jasmine's back as he pushed open the front door. "Dad tanned my hide and I never did it again, but I found other ways to torture them."

"Should I ask?"

"It's probably better if you don't. I wouldn't want to ruin your opinion of me. Better set the alarm before we head out."

Outside, dusk painted the sky in shades of purple and turned the lake from blue-green to deep black. Jasmine took a deep lungful of cold air, the pounding ache in her head easing a little as she followed Eli to his SUV. Before the accident, winter had been her favorite season. The cool grays and shadowy blues. Nothing could be hidden against the crisp white of a New England snowfall, and in the beauty of the winter landscape Jasmine had found a kind of peaceful contentment.

Now she tried not to dwell on the starkness of the leafless trees or the dead gray of the sky. Those things only reminded her of loss and loneliness, and she really didn't need any reminders of those things.

"Has Sarah thawed at all since this morning?" Eli's question pulled Jasmine from her thoughts, and she shook her head.

"Only when I mentioned you."

"Glad I could be of some use." He gestured her into the SUV, then strode around to the driver's side and got in. "At least she's out having fun with a friend. That's got to be an improvement over the past couple of weeks."

"True. Another month or so and she'll be back to her old self and able to get along on her own."

"And then you'll go back home?"

"That's the plan." Though returning to her empty cottage held a lot less appeal now than it had a few days ago. "How about you? What will you do once you find Rebecca?"

"I've got a few World War II veterans to hook up with in Bedford. I'm doing an article on their lives post-war."

"So you'll stay around here for a while?"

"A good month or so. Unless it takes me longer than that to find Rebecca."

"You think it will?"

"I don't know. I hope not. For Marcus's sake. Personally, I've found a lot to like about Lakeview and a couple of good reasons to stick around, so I'm not in that big of a hurry to leave."

He didn't elaborate and Jasmine didn't ask him to. She wasn't sure she wanted to know what he meant, or what or who those good reasons for sticking around might be.

They pulled into the parking lot of Fellowship Community Church just shy of the seven o'clock potluck's official kick-off. Eli figured that was pretty good timing, though Mom and Gran would have had something to say about the store-bought potato salad that he'd grabbed from a grocery-store deli. Home cooked was the way to go in situations like this. Especially if you wanted to make an impression. And he did want to do that.

"Well, here we are." Jasmine didn't sound happy about it, and Eli wondered again if he should have insisted she stay home. He'd planned to. When he'd walked into Sarah's house and seen Jasmine's tear-tracked cheeks and bloodshot eyes, he'd decided then and there that she wasn't coming to the church.

Somehow that had all changed and here they were. Here *she* was. He still hadn't decided how it had happened. "You sure you're up to this? I can take you back to the house if you want."

"And miss out on the excitement of overcooked casseroles

and stale chips? I don't think so." She smiled, but there was a vague unease to her expression, as if she weren't quite sure she was doing the right thing.

"Overcooked casseroles and stale chips? You haven't been to the right potlucks." He wrapped his hand around hers, feeling the delicate bones of her fingers, the softness of her skin. Strong, tough, but fragile in a way he hadn't expected when he'd seen her that first day.

"I've been to plenty of them. Our church has one every Wednesday. It's always the same thing—taco salad, macaroni and beef, lasagna, a few other pasta dishes. All lukewarm and overcooked."

"Come down my way sometime and I'll show you the true meaning of potluck."

"Not store-bought potato salad?" She nodded toward the brown paper bag he carried.

"Mom and Gran would disown me if they found out I'd brought this to church. No. Where I come from it's homemade the right way. Buttery rolls, creamy potatoes, fried chicken."

"Heart attack on a plate?"

"Oh yeah. And what a way to go." His hand tightened on hers as they moved toward the church, the unconscious gesture one he recognized for what it was. He was falling for Jasmine and he wasn't sure what to do about it. Tonight wasn't the time to decide, though.

Several couples were filing into the church ahead of Jazz and Eli, carrying plastic-covered containers, speaking in hushed tones as they moved into the building. It should have been a relaxed scene, but Eli felt no peace. Instead, he felt anxious, his spirit uneasy.

There was something wrong, something ugly and dark that he couldn't quite put his finger on, but that he was sure had something to do with Rebecca's disappearance. The sermon he'd heard McKenna preach had been Biblically based and, at its core, made good theological sense. Eli hadn't found much to gripe about in it, but he'd still worried it over in his head for the past few days. Maybe it was the messenger rather than the message that he found disturbing.

"Eli, it's good to see you again. And Jasmine, wasn't it?" Reverend McKenna stepped toward them, and Eli was sure Jasmine flinched. Obviously, she felt as comforted by the reverend's presence as he did.

"Yes. It's good to see you again, too, Reverend." To her credit, Jasmine didn't sound uneasy or afraid. "I hope the invitation to the potluck is still open."

"Of course. Is your mother-in-law feeling well enough to be left alone?"

"She's out with a friend. I thought I should get out, too."

"Wonderful. We're in the fellowship hall. It's small and outdated, but meets our needs. I've got an emergency at the hospital, but I'm sure the rest of the congregation will welcome you. Follow me. I'll take you downstairs before I leave."

He led them through a narrow hallway and down into a claustrophobic basement filled with tables, the heavy scent of food only making the air seem thicker. For a moment, Eli spun back in time, lying under the wreckage of the truck he'd been riding in, unable to move, his leg pulsing blood. Trapped. Dying.

"Hey, are you okay?" Jasmine squeezed his hand, her warmth anchoring him to the present.

"Great, but looking at the layout on the buffet table, I'd say your idea about the food was more on target than mine."

"Let's put the stuff you brought down." She scanned his face as she spoke, and must have seen some hint of the memories he carried because she squeezed his hand again, offering him a sweet smile that pretty much wiped out anything else in his head.

"Good idea. Then we'll mingle."

"Mingle? With whom? Everyone seems more intent on the food than on the company."

She was right. Eli had been to a lot of potlucks in his day, but none had been quite this quiet. He leaned close, whispering in her ear. "There are a few people talking at the table near the wall. Let's sit there."

Before they could move in that direction, Mary's parents walked into the room. Jackson met Eli's eyes and scowled, turning in the opposite direction. Laura moved toward them, a hopeful smile creasing her face. "You came! I'm so glad. Come sit at the table with Jackson and me."

"I'm not sure your husband—"

"Don't worry about Jackson. He's more bark than bite." Her smile was brittle, but her eyes flashed with determination. If she knew something about Rebecca, she'd share it if it meant finding out news about her daughter. For that, Eli was willing to risk Jackson's unhappiness.

He smiled, switching directions and pulling Jasmine with him. "Then let's go."

FIFTEEN

Jackson and Laura wouldn't have been Jasmine's choice of dinner partners, but short of pulling away from Eli and finding another table, there wasn't much she could do about it. A plate piled high with overcooked pasta in one hand and a glass of iced tea in the other, she settled into a seat across from Laura, doing her best to smile amicably as she met her gaze. "Thanks again for inviting us tonight."

"Thank you for coming."

"Would have been better if they hadn't." Jackson grumbled the words just loud enough for Jasmine to hear. She decided to ignore him, scooping up a bite of mushy noodles mixed with tuna and wishing she'd stayed home.

"Why is that?" Eli forked up the same tuna surprise, swallowing it down as he focused his attention on Jackson.

"We don't take too kindly to people who want to bring their modern thinking into our community."

"I'm not sure I'm following."

"Sarah Hart has a lot of opinions about the way a home should be run. Those ideas aren't something we want our young indoctrinated in. If you've got the same ideas, it might be best if you leave now." Jackson shoveled down food as if he hadn't eaten in a month, and Jasmine's stomach rebelled at the sight.

"I can't believe that Sarah would try to indoctrinate anyone with any ideas."

"Then you don't know her very well." Jackson swigged a glass of soda and eyed Jasmine over the rim. "Much as we were sorry to hear of her accident, we couldn't help thinking she got her just desserts."

"Jackson!" Laura's face burned red as several people at the table focused their attention on the conversation.

"It's the truth, and you know it. The woman put herself in our place and God punished her for it."

"She says someone else was responsible for the *punishment*. Maybe you know who that was." Eli spoke quietly, but his words seemed to carry. Several people at other tables were now tuning in, wide eyed and curious.

"Are you accusing me of something?"

"Just asking."

"I had nothing to do with Sarah's accident, and I don't know of anyone who did."

Eli shrugged, taking a few more bites of food as if he hadn't a care in the world. In the quiet that followed, Laura leaned toward Jasmine. "Did you ask Sarah about Mary?"

"I did, but she wouldn't tell me anything." The fact that she'd given Eli contact information wasn't something Jasmine could share. Not with so many people around and not after what Sarah had said to her.

"Oh. I was hoping…" She smiled brightly, tears obvious in her eyes. "But thank you for trying. I'm sure Mary will come home when she's ready."

"Do you think Rebecca will? Come home, I mean." Eli asked the question so casually even Jasmine, who'd been expecting it, almost missed it.

"Rebecca?" Jackson shook his head. "She won't be

coming back. Place was too backcountry for her. Told the reverend that more times than I can count."

"You actually heard her say that?"

"I didn't have to. Reverend McKenna told me in confidence and asked me to pray with him about it. Of course, at the time, he was hoping she'd come around to this way of life."

"It's disappointing that she couldn't." Eli's statement was open ended, just begging Jackson to fill in more information. Jasmine could imagine him interviewing people for the articles he wrote, his steady gaze and easy tone encouraging confidence.

"Very disappointing. After losing his first wife in such a tragic way, we were all praying that he'd find another woman to love. Someone who would be with him forever." Laura sighed, and a few of the other women at the table nodded agreement.

"I heard Rebecca was a nice woman with a very strong faith." Again, Eli spoke into the lull, prodding the conversation along in the direction he wanted it to go.

"She seemed it. We all liked her, and had high hopes for what she'd bring to the ministry. It's hard for a shepherd to guide his sheep without a helpmate to offer support."

"Then that must have made her leaving doubly hard to bear."

Jackson shrugged. "Better for her not to be here if she couldn't conform to the way of life we've striven for."

"What way would that be?"

"Submission and respect for authority are paramount here. Men and women must subject themselves to the authority over them." Jackson continued on in that vein, and Jasmine wondered if it was a pet subject. One he rehearsed regularly.

"Have things been going okay for your mother-in-law?" Laura leaned toward Jasmine, speaking quietly so as not to interrupt her husband.

"She's recovering. It'll be a while before she's completely herself, though."

"I was so sorry to hear about her accident. Despite what my husband said, we really don't believe she deserved what happened."

"Thank you for saying so."

"The thing is, Jackson and Mary were very close. This is hurting him terribly and he'd much rather blame someone else than blame his own poor decisions."

"What do you mean?"

Laura's cheeks heated again, and she shook her head. "I'm just rambling. Ignore me."

"But—"

"You haven't eaten very much." Laura cut her off, obviously unwilling to discuss the subject further.

"I'm not very hungry."

"There's a trash can by the buffet table, if you'd rather not finish."

"Thanks." Jasmine grabbed her plate and stood, glad to be away from the oppressive atmosphere of the table.

"Hello." A woman strode up beside her as she dumped her plate, smiling shyly, her dark eyes and dark hair striking against very pale skin. Thin, but for a visible pregnancy, she seemed frail and very young.

"Hi."

"You're Sarah Hart's daughter-in-law, aren't you?"

"That's right."

"I'm Niki Morgan. Mary and I are good friends."

"It's nice to meet you, Niki."

"I was hoping to come out and visit Mrs. Hart after her accident, but my husband doesn't want me driving when I'm so pregnant." She patted her stomach, smiling a little. "How is she doing?"

"Better."

"I'm glad. Mary only had good things to say about her. I think she thought getting that job with Mrs. Hart was the best thing to ever happen to her."

"I'll tell Sarah you said so."

"Will you also tell her that if she talks to Mary she should tell her Niki is doing great, and that I miss her?"

"I will."

"Thanks. I—"

"Nicole, we'd better get home and rested up. It won't do for you to get too tired so close to the baby's arrival." A man who looked to be in his mid-to-late thirties strode toward them, his face ruggedly handsome but more worn than his much younger bride. "I hope you'll excuse us. My wife has had a difficult pregnancy. She really does need her rest."

"Of course." They strode away, and Jasmine glanced back toward the table, looking for Eli. He'd stood and was moving toward her, his nearly empty plate in hand, his gaze assessing as he moved closer.

"Are you doing okay?"

"Great. How about you?" She forced an upbeat smile, knowing they were being observed.

"Good." He leaned close. "If I haven't gotten a fatal dose of food poisoning from the tuna casserole."

Jasmine laughed, relaxing for the first time since they'd arrived. "Are we going back to the table?"

"No. People are starting to loosen up. I figure we'll go around and chat for a bit."

"Okay."

"And when we're done, I'll take you out for some real food." The last was spoken close to her ear, his lips brushing her skin, the feel of them shivering through her and making her want to turn into his arms, wrap herself in his strength.

She stepped back, refusing to give in to temptation. "Where to first?"

"Let's start with the closest table and work our way around the room."

She grimaced, but moved toward the table with him. She might not want to chat with the entire roomful of people, but it would be worth it if it meant she could escape the claustrophobic basement sooner rather than later.

It was later, much later, by the time they finally finished introducing themselves and chatting with each and every person in attendance. The headache Jasmine had thought she was rid of was pounding behind her eyes with a vengeance, her nearly empty stomach rumbling in protest as they moved up the basement steps and outside into the crisp night air.

Finally. Freedom.

"You look as relieved as I feel." Eli opened the door to the SUV, and Jasmine climbed in.

"I can't remember the last time I've been so happy to get something over with."

"I can. I'd played a prank on the elementary-school principal and Dad decided it would be a good idea for me to apologize in front of the entire school."

"No way."

"It's true. He called the school, arranged for there to be an assembly the following morning. I didn't sleep a wink the entire night."

"That was a pretty harsh punishment."

"Not when you consider the crime."

"Which was?"

"I called the police and told them Mr. Beasley had a gun in his desk drawer."

"What? Why?"

"Because he did. It was a water pistol I'd brought to school and I wanted it back."

"How old were you?"

"Five."

"A baby."

"Old enough to know better, and to apologize in front of the entire school." He started the car, pulled out of the parking lot. "Fortunately, Mr. Beasley was a forgiving kind of guy. He didn't hold it against me and the next five years went off without a hitch. At least that's my story."

"Your parents have a different one?"

"It might vary a bit from mine." He flashed a grin, his teeth gleaming white in the darkness of the SUV. "Come on. Let's put this place behind us and go get some real food. There's a diner in Lakeview that's probably still open."

Dinner at a restaurant? That seemed a little too much like a date for comfort. "I'm not very hungry."

Her stomach growled loudly enough to be heard in the next county over, and Jasmine was glad the darkness hid her burning cheeks.

"Since it would be ungentlemanly of me to point out that your stomach is rumbling louder than summer thunder, I'll just say that I'm hungry, and if it wouldn't put you out, I'd really like to stop for something to eat."

Jasmine laughed, the sound bubbling up and spilling out before she realized it was there. "I guess I can't say no."

"I guess you can't." He started the engine and pulled away from the church, his hands tight around the steering wheel. Up until now, Jasmine had thought he was relaxed and at ease. Except for that first moment when they'd stepped down into the basement, Eli had acted as if he belonged at Fellowship Community. Now his tension was obvious in the taut line of his mouth and jaw.

"I'm sorry we didn't learn more about Rebecca tonight."

"We learned more than what we knew before. The people at Fellowship Community liked and admired Rebecca. Until she disappeared, they thought she was a responsible, respectable, God-fearing woman."

"That doesn't help us find her."

"No, but it confirms what we already suspected. It would be out of character for Rebecca to pursue a relationship with a man who wasn't her husband."

"People do step out of character sometimes."

"They do. What we need to know is if Rebecca did."

"I guess you have an idea about how we can find out."

"I wish I did. I've been to the college, but couldn't find any students who remembered Rebecca. The one professor Marcus knew of only remembered her as a good student who was more interested in her studies than in socializing."

"What was her major?"

"She was pursuing a master's in education."

"Maybe you could contact the head of the education department."

"I did. The school's got a privacy policy and he's not willing to talk about Rebecca."

"The police—"

"Their hands are tied. There's no evidence of foul play and no reason to believe McKenna is lying."

"Except that Rebecca hasn't contacted her brother."

"Except that." He pulled into the parking lot of Becky's Diner. A small restaurant on Main Street, it was a popular hangout for Lakeview residents. Jasmine had been there many times with John and the girls, laughing and relaxing over meals or ice cream. The memory of those times hung in the air as she followed Eli to the door and stepped into the diner.

"Jasmine Hart! As I live and breathe! I never did think I'd see you in here again." The proprietress of the restaurant hurried across the dining room, her dark eyes flashing with pleasure. Doris ran the establishment with a firm hand, though her employees and customers knew her gruff exterior hid a compassionate heart.

"I was in the other morning picking up some éclairs for Sarah."

"So I heard from Patti. Come on. Sit down. You've gotten too skinny. You need to eat." She turned her attention to Eli. "I'll feed you, too, while I'm at it."

"I appreciate that, Ms. Doris, seeing as how I'm paying for the meal." Eli grinned, and Doris swatted him on the arm as if they were old friends.

"Already sassing me, and we've only known each other a week. You'll be lucky if I feed you at all. Now sit. I'll be back in five with some strong coffee."

"She's like a mini-tornado." Eli spoke quietly as Doris moved away.

Jasmine nodded, staring down at the menu and trying not to feel uncomfortable. How could she feel anything else, though? Her first date with John had been here. Every birthday that they'd celebrated in Lakeview had ended in one of Doris's booths, nibbling pie and laughing over coffee. She swallowed back the thought and tried to answer past the lump in her throat. "Doris has been like that as long as I've known her. I don't know where she gets the energy."

"I'd take half of it. Barring that, I'll settle for a meatloaf-and-potato dinner."

"That does sound good." She read the list of entrées on the menu, but the words were blurry and as fast as she took them in, she forgot them again. Her heart thudded painfully in her chest, and her breath seemed to catch in her lungs.

"Then why do you look like you're about to hop out of that chair and run for the door?"

"It's been a long few days. I guess I'm just exhausted."

"Somehow I'm thinking that's not the entire truth."

There was nothing she could say to that. Nothing she was willing to say, anyway.

"Jasmine?" He tilted her chin up with his finger, the contact spreading heat along her jaw. "Tell me what's wrong."

"Nothing." She shrugged, tried to smile. "It's just been a while since I've had dinner with a man."

She thought he'd make light of the comment, try to put her at ease, but he leaned close, covering her hand with his, his eyes the deep-gold of a fall sunset. "I'll tell Doris we've changed our minds."

"No. It's okay. I'm just being silly."

"You could never be that. Beautiful, intelligent, interesting, but not silly."

She blushed three shades of red, and probably would have said something inane if Doris hadn't shown up with the coffee. "Black and strong just like you like it, Jazz. Same for you, Eli." She set both cups down on the table and pulled an order pad from her pocket. "Know what you want yet?"

"Just a salad." Jazz wasn't sure she could choke down anything more than that.

"Salad?" Doris raised an eyebrow, but didn't comment further. "How about you, Eli?"

"The meat-loaf plate."

"Mashed potatoes?"

"Is there any other kind?"

"Beans?"

"Sure."

"And a salad." She jotted the last down without waiting for Eli's consent. "Be back in a few."

Was it time for small talk? A discussion of the weather? More exchanges of ideas about Rebecca's whereabouts? What did women and men talk about when they went to dinner together?

As if he sensed her thoughts, Eli squeezed her hand. "Relax. It's just dinner."

"Maybe to you. To me, it's…"

"What?

"One step further away from what I used to be." A wife. A mother.

"You'll always be what you were. You're just adding something new to it."

"I don't want anything new, Eli. I just want what I had."

"I wish I could give it to you." His thumb stroked her knuckles, his gaze so warm and steady she wanted to sink into it.

"Do you always know the right thing to say?"

"Not nearly enough." He smiled, releasing her hand as Doris approached with a tray of food.

"Salads." She set one in front of Jasmine, one in front of Eli, and then put a plate piled high with meat loaf and potatoes in front of Jasmine.

"Actually, this is Eli's."

"Do I look daft? If it were his, I would have put it in front of him." She set another plate in front of Eli. "Eat. Both of you." She speared Jasmine with the kind of look that probably took years to perfect and walked away.

"Guess you're going to have to eat."

"I guess I am." Jasmine picked up the fork and shoveled up a mouthful of potatoes, hoping she wouldn't choke on them. No matter what Eli said, she couldn't quite shake the feeling that every minute she spent with him was a minute further away from the life she'd lived with John and her daughters.

SIXTEEN

Despite her feelings, Jasmine managed to relax and enjoy the hour she and Eli spent at Becky's Diner. The food was good, the conversation great, and it all had the added benefit of taking place outside the oppressive atmosphere of Sarah's house.

By the time Eli pulled the SUV up in front of the rancher, Jasmine was feeling more relaxed than she had in a long time. "Thank you for dinner, Eli."

"It was the least I could do after torturing you with that potluck food."

"You didn't torture me. Those poor women who cooked the food did." They walked up the porch steps together, and Jasmine unlocked the door, turning to disarm the alarm. "That's funny."

"What?"

"I was sure I turned the alarm on."

"Didn't you?"

"It's not on now."

"Could you have forgotten?" Eli stepped into the house, his shoulder brushing Jasmine's as he leaned forward to look at the security panel.

"I don't think so. I have a security system in New Hampshire. I'm a stickler for making sure it's on before I leave, but who knows? The past few days have been hectic and I'm way overtired. Maybe I did forget to set it."

"Tell you what. You get back in my car, and I'll take a look around. See if there's anything suspicious in the house." Or anyone.

Eli didn't say the words, but Jasmine was pretty sure he was thinking them. "Are you kidding? I'm not going to sit outside alone in the dark when some unknown bad guy might be hanging around. I'm coming with you."

"I don't think that's a good idea." Eli's tone was icy and clipped, his expression set in stone.

Jasmine didn't care. No matter what he said, she wasn't going back outside. "I do. And since I'm a thirty-three-year-old woman, I think I'm capable of making the decision myself."

His eyes flashed bronze fire, but he didn't argue further. Instead, he moved deeper into the house, flicking on lights in the living room, the kitchen, the hall. Jasmine shadowed him, walking so close that she could feel the heat of his body and the tension rolling off him. He shoved the door to Sarah's room open, pulled open her closet door, glanced under the bed. Jasmine hovered in the doorway, her heart slamming a hard, sickening beat. Was someone in the house? Hiding? Waiting? Ready to pounce?

Two minutes later, they'd looked in every room and closet, peeked under beds and checked the locks on the windows and doors. Everything seemed fine, nothing touched, moved or otherwise out of place.

Jasmine knew she should breathe a sigh of relief, say good-night to Eli and get on with the evening, but something felt off, and she couldn't shake the feeling that things weren't as okay as they seemed. "I guess I did forget to set the alarm."

"Maybe."

"Why else would it be off? Sarah and I are the only people who have the code, and Sarah's out with Germaine."

"I don't know, but I don't like it." He raked a hand over his short-cropped hair and scowled. "Here's what I'm thinking. Probably you forgot to turn the alarm on. On the off chance you didn't and someone has access to the code, we need to reset it."

"That should be easy enough to do."

"Yeah, let's just hope it keeps you and Sarah safe."

As Jasmine reset the code, Eli paced the living room, moving from one window to the next, pulling back the curtains and looking out into the night until Jasmine wanted to cross the room, put her hands on his shoulders and hold him still.

"You're making me a nervous wreck, Eli."

He stopped, then turned to face her, a half smile playing at the corners of his mouth. "Sorry about that. A year out of the military and I'm still looking for trouble around every corner."

"It's okay. I was on edge before you started pacing the floor."

"How about we call the sheriff? Have him come out and look around."

"And tell him what? That I thought I set the alarm, but when I got home it was off and the house was exactly the way I left it? I don't think that's something to drag him out here for." Jasmine shook her head, leaning her shoulder against the wall, the headache she'd been fighting all night back in full force.

"Maybe not, but it would make me feel better." He crossed the room, smoothing his hands up her arms so that they rested on her shoulders. Despite the thickness of her sweater, she could feel the heat of his palms, the firm strength of his fingers. So different than John's long, thin hands. Yet somehow comfortingly familiar.

She blinked, shoving away the thought, wishing she had

the gumption to move aside. But Eli's touch was as welcome as a warm spring breeze after a frigid winter and she stayed right where she was, enjoying it. "I'll be okay. I've been living alone for three years. One more night isn't going to make a difference."

"Maybe I should sack out on the couch. Just in case."

"In case what? No one is after me, Eli. If something is going on, it's Sarah who is involved."

"Just keep the doors and windows locked and the alarm on. I'd hate for anything to happen to you." He leaned down, leaned in. So close she could see specks of green in his eyes, could feel the warmth of his breath against her lips, and knew beyond a shadow of a doubt what he intended.

He was going to kiss her.

Kiss her?!

Back away.

Move closer.

Tell him no.

Tell him yes.

A million thoughts screamed through her mind, and before Jasmine could sort through them, Eli's lips brushed against hers, the touch so tender, so gentle it was barely there. Somehow, though, that light touch filled her with longing and sent a cold, hard shaft of grief through her heart.

John. What would he think if he knew she was moving on with her life? Moving away from what they'd built together? Letting their dreams fly off.

"It's okay." Eli's palms swept down her cheeks, brushing away the moisture she hadn't known was there.

"I know." But she didn't. Not really. Because it didn't feel okay. It felt like betrayal.

She stepped back, forcing herself to meet Eli's eyes. "It's getting late."

"I guess that's my cue to leave." His smile was as gentle as his kiss had been.

"Thanks for checking out the house for me."

"Thanks for coming to the potluck." He opened the door, stepped out into the darkness. "Lock the door. Set the alarm."

"I will."

"Good night, Jasmine."

"Good night." She closed the door, locked it, set the alarm.

Eli had kissed her.

She'd let him.

It shouldn't have mattered so much to her, but it did. A kiss. So simple. So completely life altering.

She shook her head, walking through the house, rechecking all the areas she and Eli had already walked through. If only she could understand God's plans for her life. She'd once thought she did. Marry John, raise children with him, write her books and live her life. It had been easy to see those things stretching out for thirty, forty, fifty years into the future.

That hadn't been how it had worked out though. Asking why not was a waste of energy. What she knew for sure was that she wouldn't risk her heart again.

The phone rang as she settled onto her bed, the sound making her jump. She answered, thinking it might be Sarah calling to check in. "Hello?"

"Hey, just checking to make sure you were okay." Eli's voice filled her ear, tender and warm, and much too welcome.

"I locked the doors. The alarm is on."

"That's not what I was worried about."

"Then what?"

"I've been thinking I should apologize for kissing you, but I decided I'm not really sorry."

Despite the confusion and sadness she'd been feeling, Jasmine smiled. "And that's what you're worried about?"

"I'm worried that you'll think I'm pushing you for something you're not ready to give. That isn't my intention."

"Then what is?"

"To get to know you and to see what comes of it."

"I'm not interested in anything coming of it, Eli. I'm not *ready* for anything."

"Are you sure? Everyone needs someone in their corner. Going it alone is just too tough."

He was right about that. Being alone was her choice, but it was often a lonely one. Without someone to talk to and share ideas with, life had become a pencil drawing—all dark lines and shades of gray. "I've got people in my corner. Sarah. Friends back at home."

"And now you've got me." There was a smile in his voice, and Jasmine's heart responded, skipping a beat, racing forward.

"Eli—"

"There's always room in life for more friends. Call me if you need anything." He hung up before she could respond, and Jasmine stood up, paced across the room and pulled open the curtains.

Outside, the night was black and silent. If she pressed her face close to the glass, Jasmine was sure she could see the azalea bush that now sheltered the piece of wood she'd pried off the dock before it had been repaired. It had been a silly thing to do. Wood didn't carry memories any more than a house did. Somehow, though, Jasmine hadn't been able to let that chunk of wood go. Maybe because she knew how time could fade what the mind held dear. Fifteen years after her mother's death, Jasmine sometimes had trouble picturing her face, remembering the cadence of her voice. She didn't want that to happen with her children and with John, but maybe it had to. Maybe that was the only way to move on.

"But I don't want to move on. I want to go back." She whispered the words, wishing they had the power to change things. But only God had that, and He'd made His decision about her life and about the lives of John and the girls. They'd moved on, their journey through life ended, and she'd stayed put. Walking alone the path that used to be so crowded with love and laughter.

You don't have to be alone.

The thought wound its way through her mind, demanding her attention and refusing to depart. Eli's voice, whispering in her ear, telling her there was always room in life for more friends.

But was there room in life for second chances at happiness? Jasmine wasn't sure, but maybe she needed to find out.

She sighed, running a hand over her hair and wishing she were tired, then maybe she could fall asleep and forget her worries for a while. But she wasn't tired, so she paced back across the room, trailing her hand over the books that lined the shelves, looking for one that would hold her attention. There were plenty to choose from—all love stories and romances. Modern fairy tales. Exactly what Jasmine didn't need to read.

Disgusted, she pulled the only non-romance from the shelf—a worn New Testament that had dog-eared pages and a stained leather cover. She settled onto the edge of the bed, flipping open to the book of Matthew and skimming the nativity story. She'd read it all before, knew the details down to the horrid king who sent soldiers to kill Jewish boys. She needed something different. Some new information that would change her perspective, or at least give her some semblance of peace.

She flipped through the pages, scanning passages that had been highlighted years ago by a hand other than her own.

Bright yellow against the creamy page, the words jumping out in bold relief. Words of hope, of faith. Words that someone had believed and trusted in. She wanted to do the same; wanted to embrace faith with the same zeal as the person who'd read and marked this Bible. "I really do want to know You, Lord."

She whispered the words as she closed the Bible, smoothing the creased cover, wondering who had marked it so enthusiastically. She flipped to the first page where names and dates were listed. Birthdays. Deaths. At the top, marked in clear, bold script was John's name.

She smiled, pressing it close to her heart for just a moment before setting it down on the bedside table. It figured that this was his. Even in death he seemed determined to help her grow in faith. The truth was, though, that she'd have to find the answers she sought herself, have to learn to have a relationship with God that didn't depend on someone else's beliefs. It was all her now. And only she could determine what she believed.

She reached for the light and turned it off, settling down against the pillow, wishing for sleep, the minutes ticking into hours as the night stretched on and the silence of the house grew deeper.

Dawn stretched golden fingers across the sky as Jasmine stood on the newly constructed dock and took her fist sip of coffee. Cold brisk air stung her cheeks, doing more than the coffee to wake her. She'd fallen asleep a few hours before sunrise and had woken tired and out of sorts a couple of hours later. Soon, Sarah would be home. The two of them needed to talk. No matter how angry Sarah was and no matter how much Jasmine wanted to avoid upsetting her more, the air needed to be cleared. They were family after all. The only family either had left.

She turned away from the gray-green lake and started back up toward the house, unconsciously glancing up the distant hill toward the cabin Eli was renting. Was he awake? Maybe out running as he had been the previous day? She had the urge to walk up the hill, knock on the door and see if he was there, but it was barely seven in the morning and she doubted he'd appreciate the visit. Besides, she'd spent plenty of early mornings alone. Visiting with Eli wasn't a necessity. It wasn't even an option if she wanted to keep pretending that she wasn't attracted to him.

She shook her head, shoving open the door to the rancher and walking inside. Of course she was attracted to Eli. What woman wouldn't be? He was charming, easy to talk to, strong and protective. An honorable man, and in Jasmine's estimation there weren't many of those around. Her poor mother had proven that, finding one dishonorable man after another to date. Watching her had convinced Jasmine that being single was preferable to being in a relationship. Until she'd met John and realized that there were men in the world who could be trusted and counted on. She'd thought he would be her one and only love, but being with Eli made her wonder if it was possible to have more than one great love in a lifetime.

The thought didn't sit well, and she shoved it away as she toasted a piece of bread and slathered it with butter and jam. Sugar. A surefire way to get the brain functioning again.

She'd just taken her first bite when the telephone rang. She grabbed it, glancing at the Caller ID and wondering who'd be calling so early. Germaine's number popped up, and her heart jumped, worry turning the jelly toast to dust in her mouth. "Hello?"

"Jasmine, Germaine here. I'll be there in an hour to pick Sarah up. I'm just calling to make sure she dragged herself out of bed."

"Sarah?" Obviously, Jasmine wasn't awake yet because nothing Germaine was saying made sense.

"Of course Sarah. Who else?"

"But she's with you."

"No, she's not. I dropped her off last night. She felt so bad about the argument you two had, she insisted on going back to the house and apologizing. Course the fact that I told her how stubborn and pigheaded she was had a lot to do with that."

"What time did you drop her off?" Jasmine walked toward Sarah's room as she spoke. Maybe her mother-in-law had come home during those few hours that Jasmine had slept.

"Around eight last night. I wasn't too happy about it, either. The way I see it, you make a commitment to something, you follow through. We were supposed to watch a couple of comedies. Laughter is good for the soul, you know."

"So they say." Jasmine glanced in Sarah's room, her blood running cold as she saw the empty bed.

"So, is she awake? I don't want to miss the early bird special at the diner."

"No. She's not awake, Germaine. She's not even here. I've got to go. I need to call the police." She hung up, then dialed the sheriff's department, her hands trembling, her stomach churning. The security system had been turned off. If only she'd thought more about it, maybe she would have realized that Sarah had returned home. That she'd somehow disappeared.

But Jasmine hadn't, and now all she could do was wait and pray, hoping that once the sheriff arrived, he'd be able to find out exactly what had happened to Sarah.

SEVENTEEN

Eli's phone rang as he finished tying his running shoes. The interruption was unexpected, but welcome. Anything to keep from having to go out in the cold. He grabbed the phone expecting to hear his mother's or father's voice. Maybe one of his sisters.

Instead, Jasmine's voice filled his ear, the panic in it making his pulse race and his stomach twist. "Sarah's gone."

"What do you mean, gone? She's at Germaine's house, right?" He glanced at the clock; it was a little before seven. Too early for Sarah to have returned home.

"She came home last night. Germaine just called. I have to go. The police... I really have to go." She hung up, and Eli's mind filled with possibilities. Had Sarah returned home and been kidnapped by someone? Had Jasmine been attacked? Or had Sarah come home last night and been grabbed before he and Jasmine had returned to the house?

He didn't bother with a coat, just raced out into the gray morning, jumping into the SUV and speeding down the hill toward the rancher. In the distance, sirens were screaming. Help was on the way, but was it too late? How many hours had it been since Sarah had returned home? Ten? Twelve? More?

He should have insisted Jasmine call the sheriff the

previous night. Should have sensed that something was wrong. But he hadn't and there was nothing he could do now but pray that Sarah was okay.

The door to the house flew open as he pulled up, and Jasmine raced outside, her feet bare, her long-sleeved T-shirt clinging to her frame. Hair a wild halo of curls around her strong, determined face, she looked tough. Ready for whatever would come. But her eyes gave her away. Worry and fear shouted from their depths, turning green-blue to stormy gray, and making Eli want to pull her close, tell her everything was going to be okay.

"I'm sorry. I shouldn't have called. I realized that after. I just..." Her voice trailed off, and she shrugged, her gaze fixed on the road as if she could will the sheriff to appear.

He ignored her comments and gave in to his instincts, tugging Jasmine into his arms, feeling the tremors that coursed through her. "It's going to be okay."

"I don't think so, Eli. I really don't. She's been gone all night. Anything could have happened."

"That doesn't mean it did. There could be an explanation."

"Like what? She can barely walk, let alone drive. Besides, her car is in the garage. She didn't go anywhere. At least not on her own."

"Maybe another friend came by and picked her up."

"She would have left me a note."

"She was angry with you. Maybe she didn't want to do that."

"We can circle around it as much as we want, Eli, but the truth is something happened to Sarah. And I don't mean she decided to go somewhere with a friend." The fear in Jasmine's voice was unmistakable, and her entire body shook with it, but she pulled away from his embrace, pacing across the porch, oblivious to the frozen wood beneath her bare feet.

"We're going to find her."

"But will she be alive when we do?"

"Yes."

"You have more faith than I do." She ran a hand over her curls, shook her head. "I never should have let her go with Germaine."

"She's an adult, Jasmine. She made up her mind to go and there was nothing you could do to stop her."

"But I could have tried to. I could have told her I needed her here. I could have been honest about not wanting to be alone in the house. Then none of this would have happened."

"You're taking responsibility for something that isn't your fault."

"Of course it is. First I let my husband and children down. Now I've let Sarah down." Her eyes widened, and she looked stricken by the words, as if she'd never intended to say them and was surprised that they'd escaped.

"Your husband and daughters died because of someone else's mistake. Not yours."

"But I should have been with them. Just like I should have been here with Sarah last night."

"Jasmine—"

"Talking about it isn't going to help. The only thing that will help is finding out who took Sarah and where they brought her. And that's exactly what I'm going to do." She whirled toward the house, nearly running through the open doorway and down the hall that led to her bedroom.

He wanted to go after her, ask exactly what she had planned, but the sheriff's car was racing up the driveway. He waited until Jake Reed stepped out of the car, then started down the porch stairs.

"I'd say good morning, but it doesn't seem like it is one." Reed's grim words echoed Eli's thoughts. Much as he wanted to believe otherwise, he knew Jasmine was right. There was no way Sarah had gone off of her own volition.

"Jasmine's in the house. She should be back out shortly."

"She said Sarah's been missing since last night." It wasn't a question, but Eli answered anyway.

"I dropped Jasmine off around nine. Sarah was supposed to be at a friend's house, but it seems that she returned home last night around eight. No one has seen her since then."

"Nothing was out of place when you got here?"

"The alarm was off and Jasmine thought she'd set it, but everything was in order here, so we assumed she'd forgotten."

"I'd have assumed the same." He paused, glancing over his shoulder at a dark sedan that was racing toward them. "Looks like we've got company. If I'm not mistaken that's Germaine Walker's car."

"She's the friend Sarah was supposed to be with last night."

Jake nodded, but his attention was focused on the car and the woman who was stepping out of it. She was visibly shaken, her face drained of color.

"Did you find her? Was she just sleeping in another room?"

"I'm afraid not. Can you tell me the exact time you dropped her off, Germaine?"

"Around eight. She and Jasmine had a big blowout about something. Sarah said things she regretted. Our Wednesday-night prayer meeting was focusing on forgiveness, and it hit Sarah hard. She wanted to come right home and clear the air with Jasmine. She sent me off as soon as we got here. Said she wanted to spend some time praying about things."

"And she was locked in the house when you left?"

"Yes. I watched her walk in."

"I'll make some coffee." Eli stepped into the house, started a pot, paced the small kitchen, then finally gave up any pretense of not caring and moved down the hall to knock softly on Jasmine's door.

"You okay?"

"Hold on." She swung the door open, and he saw that she'd changed from jeans and a T-shirt to cargo-style black pants and a cable-knit sweater. Her hair was pulled back in a neon-yellow headband, leaving the sharp angles of her face and the delicate line of her neck exposed.

"You going somewhere?"

"Yeah. Fellowship Community. I want to have a talk with Jackson Cornell."

"I'm thinking that might be better left for the sheriff."

"I'm not sitting around here waiting for things to happen. I'm going to find the answers I need." She moved past him, her shoulders tight, her lips set in a grim line. She meant what she was saying, but so did he. No way was he going to let her head off to Fellowship Community by herself.

"Fine. I'll go with you."

"That's not necessary."

"What's not necessary?" The sheriff strode into the living room, his gaze resting on Eli for a moment before he turned his attention to Jasmine.

"Nothing."

"Jasmine wants to go speak with a member of Fellowship Community."

They spoke in unison, and Reed raised an eyebrow. "Let's all have a seat and discuss this before we start running hog wild through the town searching for suspects."

Germaine hovered behind him, nodding her head, her eyes wide and frightened. "The sheriff is right, Jazz. You can't run off searching for Sarah without a plan."

"I have a plan. I'm going to make Jackson tell me what he knows."

"Is there a reason why you suspect him?" Reed took out a notebook and started jotting in it.

"Yes. There is."

It didn't take long for Jasmine to list all the evidence she had against Jackson. It wasn't much. She'd admit that, but since it was all she had, she planned to act on it. With or without the sheriff's approval.

"You do realize we don't have any proof that there's foul play involved in Sarah's disappearance." He spoke quietly, his dark blue eyes filled with compassion.

"What else could it be?"

"She might have decided she needed some time away. Maybe she went off with another friend."

"She wouldn't do that."

"Maybe not, but we need to check all the possibilities. Do you know her friends? We can start calling around."

"I do. I'll get started making the calls right away." Germaine jumped up, bustling with energy, determined, it seemed, to follow along with the sheriff's plan.

Jasmine wasn't quite so enthusiastic. It was possible Sarah had gone to stay with another friend, but not likely.

"Great. And I'm going to check around outside, see if there's any evidence of a struggle. You didn't find any in here, correct?" Jake asked the question, though Jasmine knew he already had an answer. Most likely, he was trying to calm her down. It wasn't working. Sarah was gone. It was her fault. She had to make it right before it was too late.

"While you're doing that, I'm heading to Fellowship Community."

"That isn't such a good idea, Jasmine." The compassion in the sheriff's eyes was gone, replaced by stony determination. "The last thing I need is two women missing."

"I know that Jackson has something to do with this."

"But you don't have evidence, and without it all you've really got is gut instinct. So, here's what's going to happen. Germaine is going to call Sarah's friends and make sure she's not with one of them. I'm going to check around outside and see if I find anything. When those two things are done, I'll head over to Fellowship Community and see what Jackson and McKenna have to say."

"By that time—"

"It's the way it's got to be. Whether any of us like it or not." The sheriff stood, moved toward the door.

"I can't sit around here waiting. I need to *do* something."

"You can pray."

Pray?

The word stuck in Jasmine's head, filled her mind, demanded attention. But she didn't want to pray, she wanted to run out the door, get in her car, follow through on her plan.

"It's going to be okay." Eli draped an arm around her shoulders, pulling her to his side, his warmth chasing away some of the chill that seemed to live in her soul.

"I really can't stay here all day waiting, Eli. I have to do something." Anything. Search the rental properties, go into town and ask around. There had to be things she could do that would help rather than hurt the sheriff's investigation.

"Then come to West Virginia with me."

"What?"

"I'm going to try and track Mary down. I can't reach her by phone. Maybe she'll be more receptive to a face-to-face visit."

"I can't leave when Sarah is missing."

"It might be for the best, Jasmine." Jake pushed open the door and stepped out onto the porch. "There's not much you can do here." Besides get in the way.

Jasmine could almost hear the last words, though the

sheriff was too professional to say them. "I can search for Sarah, and that's exactly what I plan to do."

"In that case, I'll skip my trip to West Virginia and give you a hand." Eli still had his arm around Jasmine's shoulders, and the sheriff shifted his attention from one to the other, curiosity obvious in his gaze.

He didn't comment, though, just nodded agreement. "Whatever you think is best. If you do decide to head out of town, leave me your cell-phone number so I can contact you." He headed outside, and Germaine followed close behind, already on the phone. Probably spreading the news about Sarah's disappearance as much as she was asking for information.

It wasn't a very kind thought, and Jasmine immediately regretted it. Sarah was missing and she was taking mental snipes at a woman who'd never hurt a fly. What was wrong with her?

"Come on. Let's sit down and come up with a plan of action." Eli spoke quietly as he led her back into the living room.

"I'd rather just move to the action part."

"I don't blame you, but if we do, we'll just end up wasting time."

He was right. Jasmine knew it, and she took a deep breath, trying to calm her racing heart and to still the churning ache in her stomach. "Okay. Let's plan."

"Does Sarah have an address book?"

"Yes."

"We'll start there."

"And do what?"

"Call every single person in it."

"Germaine is already making phone calls."

"She's calling mutual friends. We're going to cover all the bases."

"All right. Let's do it." She grabbed Sarah's address book from its place beside the telephone, opened up to the first page. "It's early to be calling people."

"Under the circumstances, I don't think people will mind."

He was right, but she was still hesitant. Calling and telling people Sarah was missing would make it more real than it already was, more real than Jasmine wanted it to be.

"Tell you what. How about you search Sarah's room, see if she left anything behind that you missed before. I'll start making the calls." Eli reached for the book, gently taking it from her hands.

"Eli…" She wasn't sure what she wanted to say. She didn't want to need him, but somehow she did. Her throat closed on the thought, and she couldn't speak. Instead, she walked into Sarah's room and shut the door.

Eli's low voice carried through the door as Jasmine searched the room for some clue as to Sarah's whereabouts. There was nothing. Just one photograph after another of John, the girls and Jasmine smiling into the camera. Life had been so different then. So full. So complete.

"Why, Lord? That's all I want to know. Why?" She sat on the bed, heartsick and alone.

No. Not alone.

She might not understand His ways or wisdom but she did believe God was with her. If only He'd give her the answers she needed. If only He'd bring Sarah home safely.

If only.

She blinked back tears and hurried out of the room. There wasn't time to worry and fret. She needed to act.

EIGHTEEN

10:00 p.m.

It was dark as pitch. No moonlight to reflect off the lake or lighten the trees and bushes. Jasmine stood on the back deck of the house, listening to the quiet lap of water against shore, her stomach empty and sick, her mind numb. The sheriff had been searching all day, talking to people, asking questions, but no one had seen or heard from Sarah. Without evidence of foul play, he could do no more than question Jackson and McKenna. Both had alibis for the previous night.

That left nothing but speculation. Did someone else have something against Sarah? Had the person come the previous night and taken her? Had Sarah gone for a walk, gotten hurt, fallen in the lake? A dozen men and women had spent the afternoon searching the lakeshore, checking the woods that surrounded Lakeview Retreat. Dogs had been brought in, but they'd found no scent trails other than the ones in the driveway.

Now the house had fallen silent, the searchers gone home for the night. Tomorrow, they'd start again, but Jasmine knew tomorrow wasn't soon enough. If Sarah was alive, she needed the medication the doctor had prescribed. Blood thinners. Pain pills. She needed to be found tonight. Not tomorrow.

"You need to try to get some rest." Eli spoke quietly, moving up beside her, wrapping his hand around hers.

She knew she should pull away, tell him she was fine, that he could go home, but she didn't want to be alone, and instead of doing what she should, she let her fingers link with his, let herself lean closer to his warmth.

He pressed her head to his shoulder, his hand smoothing over her hair. "Go lie down for a while, Jasmine. I'll wait by the phone in case the sheriff calls with news."

"I can't sleep when Sarah is out there somewhere."

"You'll be no good to her when she gets home if you've made yourself sick from exhaustion."

"*If* she gets home."

"She will."

"You sound a lot more confident than I feel."

"It's a matter of faith, not confidence."

"Then I wish I had as much of it as you do."

"Don't worry, I have enough for both of us."

"Funny, that's how it always was with John and me. He was so much more sure of his place in the world, of God's plan for his life than I was. He never doubted his direction. I doubted all the time."

"We're all different, Jasmine. Some of us have an easier time working on blind faith than others."

"Maybe you're right. Maybe I just need to see the path more clearly to believe in it."

"There's nothing wrong with that."

"Except for times like this when there is no path."

"There's a path. Even when you can't see it." He smoothed her hair again, his hand resting at her nape, his thumb caressing her neck.

She could have stayed there for hours, surrounded by his warmth, allowing herself to lean on his strength. That scared her more than she wanted to admit. "This isn't a good idea, Eli."

The words slipped out and he stilled, his thumb resting against the pulse point in her neck. "Isn't it?"

"I can't be vulnerable again."

"You mean you *won't* be vulnerable again."

"It's the same thing."

"No. It's not. When we decide to have a relationship with another person, we open ourselves up to hurt, disappointment and sorrow. Anyone can do that. Some people decide it's not worth it."

He was right. Of course he was, but Jasmine hadn't decided anything except that she didn't want to feel the pain of loss again. "I need to find Sarah. That's all I can think about right now."

"I've been thinking about that more and more as the day has worn on. I think the key to finding Sarah might lie with Mary."

"You think Sarah went to visit her?"

"I think Mary will be able to tell us why she left town. That might just give us the information we need to find Sarah."

"Then let's go."

"It's a little late to make a social visit."

"It isn't a social visit when you're trying to find someone you love."

Eli hesitated, then nodded. "All right. Pack an overnight bag. It's a six-hour drive, so we'll be on the road for a while. I'll get my things together and meet you back here in half an hour."

A six-hour drive? That meant they'd arrive before dawn. That was fine with Jasmine. Better to be moving forward than to be standing still waiting.

It didn't take her long to throw a change of clothes in an overnight bag, pack toiletries, pull her hair back in a headband

and slide her feet into boots. She splashed her face with water, glancing in the mirror and grimacing at what she saw there.

Genetics had been good to her, and she knew she looked younger than her years, but grief defined her as time had not. There were dark circles under eyes, her skin was a shade or two too pale, her lips leached of color. There was something indefinable as well, a worn look to her face, a hollowness in her gaze that told the real story of her life.

It was a look of defeat. One her mother had worn during the last decade of her life. One Jasmine had sworn she'd never have. She'd promised herself that she'd carve out a career, make sure she was financially independent and able to care for herself. If she married, she'd marry a man who loved her beyond measure. She would work hard to make the relationship a success, but she'd never tie her self-confidence up in it. The way she saw it, she'd either have the stable, loving relationship her mother had craved, or she wouldn't have one at all.

And she had had it. For a while.

All those dreams, all those hopes, they were from a lifetime ago. Jasmine's wishes were a lot simpler now. She wanted peace. And she wanted to find Sarah.

"Jasmine? Are you ready?" Eli interrupted her thoughts, pulling her from the past and very firmly into the present.

She stepped out into the hall, her overnight case in hand, fatigue sapping her energy even as her mind sped ahead to their meeting with Mary. Maybe she did have information that would help them find Sarah. "Ready."

Eli had his back to Jasmine, and turned as she spoke, his hair glowing gold in the hall light. He stared down into her eyes for a moment, then cupped her face in his hands. "You're exhausted, sugar. Maybe we *should* wait until morning."

Sugar? The endearment slid off his tongue as though he'd

said it a hundred times before, and Jasmine's heart jumped in acknowledgment, as if she'd heard it a hundred times before—a song she'd forgotten but now remembered again. "I'm okay."

"I don't agree. You're pushing yourself too hard."

"Everyone here today pushed themselves hard. Including you. Sarah is missing. What else are we supposed to do?"

He sighed, but didn't argue, just took the overnight case from her hand. "We may not even find Mary. You know that, right?"

"If she's not there, I can handle the disappointment. What I can't handle is sitting around here waiting for something to happen."

"All right, then. Let's go find some answers."

Jasmine followed Eli to the front door, wishing she were as confident as he seemed to be. If only she could believe that Sarah was going to be okay, that somehow they'd find her. But she didn't. She believed... She didn't know what she believed. All she could do was hope and offer up prayers she wasn't even sure were being heard.

She climbed into Eli's SUV, waiting as he dropped her overnight case on the back seat next to a duffel bag, her mind flashing to another time, another car. Another man.

"Ready?"

"How could I not be? We're getting ready to start a whole new life together." Jasmine gushed the words, her heart filled with love for the man she'd just married. John. Her friend. Her love. Her husband.

"Just the two of us." He planted a kiss on her lips, quick and light, but filled with promise.

"For now."

"Forever. Even when we have kids I'll love you like this.

With all my heart. With everything I am." His words washed over her as he drew her closer to his side.

Forever.

Only it hadn't worked out that way.

"Jasmine?" Eli squeezed her hand, his palm rough against hers. Nothing like John's soft, smooth one, but welcome and comforting.

The thought should have alarmed her, but didn't and she squeezed back, turning to face him, seeing the soft gleam of his eyes in the darkness. "Let's go."

He smiled, and pulled down the long driveway, carrying Jasmine farther and farther from Sarah's home.

And closer to whatever the future would bring.

She wasn't sure how she felt about that. All she knew was that Eli was there and she would much rather be with him than alone. "You have an address for Mary, right?"

"Shepherdstown."

"We'll arrive before dawn."

"That's the plan. If she's still there, I don't want to give her a chance to leave for the day."

"Let's hope she is there."

"I'd rather pray." Eli said the words casually, but Jasmine knew he meant them. His faith was as strong as hers was weak.

"I've tried that before."

"And?"

"And I'm never clear on God's answer. Sometimes I'll think He's leading me in one direction. Sometimes another."

"God isn't the author of confusion."

"No, but people are. We allow feelings to muddle our thoughts and confuse the issues. At least, I do." More often than she liked to admit.

"I can think of a good dozen or more times I've convinced

myself something was right when it was wrong. It always gets me in a world of trouble."

"Me, too." The last time she'd done it, she'd lost the three people she loved most in the world. The thought was a hollow ache in her heart, and she shoved it down. Not wanting to dwell on it.

Eli must have sensed the direction of her thoughts, though. He glanced her way, his gaze focused for a second before he turned it back to the road. "You're thinking about your family, aren't you?"

"I can't think of many times when I'm not."

"What happened to them wasn't your fault. You know that, right?"

"What I know is that I was supposed to be with them that day. What I know is that I had a deadline I thought couldn't wait. I let John take the girls for New Year's and promised them a great trip after my book was done. I thought it was the right decision. It was the worst one I ever made."

"You're alive because of it."

"And they're dead." Her words were harsh and angry, and she closed her mouth to keep from saying more.

"Not because of your decision, sugar. You can't really believe that."

"What else am I supposed to believe?"

"That their time here was over. That in God's plan and in His time, He brought them home."

"That's so easy to say when it isn't your family that's gone on ahead of you."

"It *isn't* easy to say, because I know how you feel. I've been there."

"Losing your friends was awful, but it isn't the same, Eli. There was nothing you could have done to prevent their deaths. Nothing that could have saved them."

"You can't know that and neither can I. I beat myself up for a year, imagining fifty different ways I could have saved them. After I was done beating myself up, I blamed God. He could have prevented it from happening. He could have spared them. He didn't. That's a hard pill to swallow."

"But you managed it."

"Sure did. After Gran shoved it down my throat and told me to stop wallowing in self-pity. 'Their lives on earth are over,' she said. 'Yours isn't. Stop asking why they died and start asking why you lived.'"

"Wow."

"Exactly. So that's what I've spent the last months doing. Asking why I lived, what I should be accomplishing. How I can honor God and the friends I lost with what I've got left of my life."

"I'm sorry, Eli. I had no idea."

"Why should you have?" He leaned forward, turned on the radio. "How about some music to keep us going?"

"Country?"

"Bluegrass."

"Let me guess, your grandmother would disown you if you played anything else."

"You've got Gran pegged all wrong. It's my dad who'd disown me. He's got his own bluegrass band." He grinned, and Jasmine smiled in return.

Being with Eli was comfortable.

Exciting.

Enjoyable.

And somehow, at least for now, that was okay.

She leaned her head back against the seat, tapping her foot to the beat as Eli headed north, carrying them closer to Mary and the answers they hoped to find.

NINETEEN

An accident on the interstate held them up for over an hour and they arrived in Shepherdstown at just past five in the morning. Small and quaint, it reminded Jasmine of her hometown in New Hampshire, its Victorian houses pressed close together with 1920s bungalows. Christmas lights still shone in a few windows, the lights glittering in multicolored splendor as Eli drove slowly through town.

"It's a pretty place." She spoke more to herself than to Eli, but he answered as he pulled into a gas-station parking lot.

"It'll be a lot prettier if we manage to locate Mary. I'm going inside to ask directions. The map search I did couldn't come up with the street."

"It must be off the beaten path."

"Way off it. Hopefully that means Mary is feeling pretty secure and hasn't run to another hiding place." He shoved open the door, grimacing a little as he got out of the car.

"Are you okay?"

"Too much driving isn't so good for my leg, but I'm fine." He smiled, but pain was obvious in his eyes, and he was limping as he moved toward the gas-station convenience store.

Jasmine hopped out her side of the car and hurried to

catch up. "You should have told me your leg was bothering you. I would have driven."

"It's not so much the driving as the sitting."

"We could have stopped and stretched."

"It wouldn't have done much good. But thanks for caring." He grinned, wrapping his arm around her waist and tugging her to his side.

"Eli—"

"You worry too much, Jasmine."

"I'm not worried."

"Sure you are. You're worried that something is happening between us. You're worried about what that might mean. You're worried I might be expecting more from you than you can give. But most of all—" he stopped walking and turned to face her "—you're worried about being hurt again."

He was so right it was scary, and Jasmine wasn't sure if she should deny the truth or admit it. "I... You're right. I am worried." And scared and anxious. For Sarah. For Mary. For Rebecca.

For herself.

"Don't be. Everything will turn out the way it's supposed to."

"That's the scary part. I don't know how it's supposed to turn out."

"So take it a day at a time and enjoy. Life flies by fast. When it's done, that's it."

"That's a maudlin thought."

"It's the truth. Being close to death brings it home loud and clear." He ran a finger down her cheek, hooked it in the collar of her sweater and tugged her closer. "And it makes a person appreciate the little things in life. Like the sound of laughter, the warmth of a hug, the sweet scent of a woman's perfume."

Jasmine's breath caught in her throat as Eli leaned closer, but she was powerless to move away. "I'm not wearing perfume."

"Then it must just be you. Sweet and subtle. Intoxicating."

"Eli—"

"I keep telling myself to give you space. I keep not listening to my own advice."

"Maybe you should."

"Do you want me to?"

"I don't know."

"That's better than no, I think." He brushed his lips against hers, just a fleeting touch but it sent warmth shivering along her spine and made her long for more.

Then he stepped away, tugged her toward the convenience store as if the kiss hadn't happened at all.

Half an hour later, they were fifteen miles outside of town, searching for a dirt road that the convenience-store clerk had assured them was there, Jasmine's thoughts spinning back to the kiss again and again. She needed to work on that. There were much more important things to be thinking about, after all. Like finding Hilltop Way and Mary. Like figuring out what had happened to Sarah.

"This is it." Eli took a sharp turn onto an unpaved road, the SUV bouncing over deep ruts and jarring Jasmine from her frustrating thoughts. She was glad. As he'd said, worry wasn't doing her any good. The best thing she could do was concentrate on the here and now, and face the rest when it came.

"How far down the road did the clerk say it was?"

"A mile. Not bad as long as my car holds together that long."

The SUV bounced again, and Jasmine slammed against the door, grabbing hold of the closest thing to her. Firm muscle beneath a cotton shirt. Warmth. Connection.

She let go as if she'd touched a hot stove, her cheeks heating, her heart doing a jittery little dance. "Sorry about that."

"What?"

"Never mind."

He chuckled and shook his head. "Relax, Jasmine. I don't bite."

But you kiss. And I'm just not ready for that.

She didn't say what she was thinking, and Eli didn't comment again, just eased off the gas so that the SUV coasted to a stop. "I think we'd better walk the rest of the way. If Mary hears us coming she may bolt."

"If she's there."

"If she's not, we haven't lost anything by being cautious." He stepped out of the car, and Jasmine did the same.

"It's darker than I thought." Her whisper barely sounded above her pounding heart, but Eli heard and moved close, grabbing her hand and leading her forward.

"Give yourself a minute. Your eyes will adjust to it and it won't seem so bad."

"I don't know about that, Eli. I'm starting to think we've made a mistake. I should have stayed home. What if Sarah returned and needed my help?"

"You know that didn't happen."

"What if the sheriff found her?"

"He would have called your cell phone."

"What—"

"There you go, worrying again. But you don't need to." He squeezed her hand, his stride purposeful, confident, as if he hadn't a doubt in the world that what they were doing was right.

Maybe it was right, but the dark morning, the tall trees that abutted the road, the creepy silence made Jasmine wonder if they'd walked out of a bad situation and straight into a worse one.

They rounded a curve in the road and a light appeared lonely and small in the darkness, gleaming softly from the ground-level window of a small ranch-style house. Bushes butted up against siding, dark blobs against the pale house. They looked like wild animals, ready to pounce on the unwary.

"Number one, Hilltop. This is it." Eli strode forward, but Jasmine grabbed his arm and pulled him to a stop.

"You're not just going to march up there and knock on the door, are you?"

"No. I'm not. You are."

"What?! No way."

"If Mary is in there, and let's assume she is, she's going to wonder who's knocking on her door this early in the morning. Maybe she won't answer. Maybe she'll decide to head out the back door in case whoever she's running from has found her."

"It's what I'd do."

"Exactly. So, I'm going around to the back door while you knock on the front. If she decides to make a run for it, I'll be there to stop her."

"What if this is the wrong house? What if Mary isn't here? What if someone else answers the door? What will I say to explain being here?" The questions spilled out, and Jasmine had to force herself to stop talking.

"You'll just tell whoever it is that there's been a family emergency and you're trying to find Mary Cornell. If they know her, that should get them talking."

"You make it sound easy."

"It is. Just have a little confidence in yourself." He gave her a gentle shove toward the door. "Count to thirty. Then knock."

"I don't know about this, Eli. Maybe I should go around to the back."

But he was already gone, disappearing around the side of the little house, blending into the shadows, leaving her to do what her common sense was screaming she shouldn't.

But this wasn't about doing what common sense demanded. This was about finding Sarah. If that meant knocking on a stranger's door, so be it.

She took a deep breath and started counting as she stepped up crumbling cement stairs to the front door. Thirty came way too fast, and she braced herself, pounding her fist against the door and waiting for a heartbeat. Then another.

A shadow moved across the lit window. Seconds later the light went out, plunging Jasmine into darkness. She hesitated, then knocked on the door again, wondering if she should call out, see if Mary was inside and would respond.

She lifted her hand to knock again, but jumped away as a loud scream rent the air. It was followed by a crack. Another scream.

Jasmine raced around the side of the house, her pulse pounding in her ears. "Eli!"

Something snagged the back of her shirt, and she was jerked to a stop. "Slow down, Jasmine. I've already been shot at. I'm not in the mood to be run over."

"Eli." Relief washed over her, and she turned to face him, her gaze going to the young woman by his side. Even in the darkness, it was obvious she was terrified, her eyes dark pools against pale skin.

"Mary?"

"No." She tugged against the grip Eli had on her arm, but he didn't release his hold.

"I think you are Mary. And I think you're way too young to be carrying a rifle."

"And I think you're a trespasser who deserves anything he gets."

"You could have killed me."

"I should have." The young woman nearly spat the words, and Jasmine decided it was time to intervene.

"I'm Jasmine Hart. My mother-in-law Sarah is missing. I was hoping to find a girl who worked for her. Mary Cornell. She may have information that will help me locate Sarah."

"Sarah's missing?" All the spit and fire seeped from the young woman's words, and she grabbed Jasmine's arm. "Since when?"

"Since yesterday."

"You'd better come inside." She hurried toward the house, and Jasmine followed, Eli close behind her.

Obviously, the woman *was* Mary.

Did she have information that would help them find Sarah? Just the thought made Jasmine's heart race. Excitement. Worry. Fear. She wasn't sure which she was feeling more of as she stepped inside the house and a light flicked on.

They were in a small kitchen, the cupboards, sink and flooring more utilitarian than attractive. A lone coffee cup sat on a nicked table. There were curtains on the window, but they were faded and old, the colors muddy rather than bright.

"I guess I should prove that my mother taught me some manners and offer you both coffee." Mary spoke into the silence, and Jasmine turned her attention to the young woman.

She didn't know what she'd been expecting. Maybe someone who looked fragile, scared and unsure. What she saw was an attractive teenager who appeared confident and self-assured. Blond. A little over average height. Slender without being skinny. Large dark eyes that somehow looked both suspicious and worried. Dark slacks, a white shirt, and a small apron tied around her waist.

"You're a waitress." Jasmine didn't know why that surprised her, or what she thought Mary would be doing to support herself.

"And a student. And if I don't leave in the next half hour, I'll be late for work. So, do you want some coffee?"

"No, thanks."

"Me, neither." Eli moved up beside Jasmine, settling a hand on her shoulder.

Mary shrugged, picked up the coffee cup and took a sip. "I'm sorry about Sarah. She was a great boss."

"We need to find her."

"You won't. He'll make sure of that." She didn't meet Jasmine's eyes as she spoke, just stared down into the coffee cup.

"Who?"

"The reverend."

"McKenna? What does he have to do with it?" Eli asked the question before Jasmine could.

"He's bad news."

"You're going to have to give us more than that."

"I can't."

"Sarah is missing, Mary. Whatever information you have, we need it."

"Look," she said, raking a hand over her hair and frowning, "Sarah helped me get a job, gave me enough money for my first month's rent on this place. She helped me get financial aid for college. She's a great lady, but I've got to think of my family."

"You think helping us will put them in danger?"

"Think it? I know it. If Reverend McKenna finds out I said anything to anyone, he'll…" Her voice trailed off and she shook her head. "Look, I wish I could help."

"You *can* help. Tell us what's going on. We'll make sure McKenna doesn't get anywhere near your family." Eli's confidence must have made an impression on Mary. She looked up from her coffee, her eyes dark and filled with fear.

"You don't know him. He can convince anyone of anything."

"You don't know us. We're not going to let anything happen to your family. Or to you. But we need your help. Without it, I'm not sure we'll find Sarah."

Mary hesitated, then collapsed into a chair. "He killed his wife."

"What?"

"Reverend McKenna killed his wife Rebecca."

"You saw him do it?"

"He *told* me he did it. He and my parents were pressuring me to marry this guy from church. Graham Mitchel. He's an elder. A nice guy, but not my type. I told them no. I wanted to get my degree, get a job, live a little before I had a family."

"There's nothing wrong with that." Jasmine sat in the chair next to Mary's, wishing she'd hurry up and tell the story, but feeling guilty for wanting to rush her. Obviously what she was saying had impacted her life.

"Not in most people's minds, but Reverend McKenna, he believes women don't need to be educated. He believes their only job should be taking care of their children and serving their husbands."

"*Serving* their husbands?" Eli met Jasmine's gaze, and she knew he was thinking the same thing she was. *Serving* was an odd word choice.

"That's what he says. I believe everything the Bible says about the relationship between a husband and wife, but I've got no plan to be a man's servant for the rest of my life."

"I don't blame you." But I really, really wish you'd tell me how this is connected to Sarah. Jasmine refrained from speaking the words that were screaming through her head, forcing herself to relax and wait.

"Yeah, well, my parents did. They kept insisting I'd be better off married and settled than getting a degree. They had the reverend over for dinner one night, and they told me if I wasn't going to cooperate they'd have to get tough. I'd been thinking all along that my parents were going to help with college. Instead, they planned to kick me out of the house unless I agreed to marry Graham."

"What'd you do?"

"I panicked. I had the job at Sarah's but it didn't pay much. I had a couple hundred dollars in my account, but not nearly enough to rent a place. So, I…" She swallowed hard, and a tear slipped down her cheek. "I went to Rebecca. I told her what was going on and asked her to talk to the reverend and to my parents. She promised that she would. That was the last time I ever saw her."

"And you think Reverend McKenna killed her?"

"I told you, I *know* he killed her. He made an announcement at church Wednesday night, told everyone that his wife had gone off with another man. I knew it wasn't true. Rebecca wasn't like that. She'd have rather stayed in a bad marriage than cheat on someone."

"And you told the reverend that?"

"Yeah. Like the idiot I am. I asked if I could speak with him privately and we went into his office." She sniffed, another tear rolling down her face. "I wasn't really thinking about Rebecca being dead. I just thought…I don't know what I thought. Maybe that he'd sent her away. Forced her to leave the same way my parents were threatening to kick me out. I told the reverend I didn't believe his story, and that

I was going to make sure everyone knew Rebecca never would have left him. Then I said something really stupid. I told him that it seemed strange that he'd been married twice and lost both his wives. He got really quiet, then he grabbed my wrist and squeezed it so hard I thought my bones would snap. He told me that if I ever said that again to anyone, he'd make me sorry I had. He said my mom could disappear just as easily as his wife had. I think if there hadn't been people out in the hall, he might have made sure *I* disappeared." She shuddered and took another sip of coffee, her hand shaking so badly brown liquid sloshed over the sides of the cup.

"So you ran?"

"I didn't even go home for a change of clothes. I just got in my car and went to Sarah's. I told her that I'd had a fight with my parents about marrying Graham and that they'd kicked me out. She called a friend here in town and got me a job, then loaned me enough money for a month's rent. I should never have pulled her into this."

"You were scared." Jasmine put her hand on Mary's shoulder, wishing she could say something comforting. But there was nothing to say. The truth was Sarah had disappeared. Just like Rebecca. Jasmine had the horrible feeling that neither woman would ever be seen again.

Hot tears filled her eyes, and she forced them back. She didn't have time to cry or mourn. Not when there was still a chance Sarah was alive. She stood, moving away from the table and Mary. "We need to call Sheriff Reed."

"I'll do it." Eli pulled out his cell phone, dialed the number.

Jasmine crossed the small room, stepped back out into the predawn, her heart aching, her throat tight, her mind filled with all the things that might have happened to Sarah.

"Not her, too, Lord. I don't want to lose anyone else." She whispered the words toward the heavens, not expecting an answer. God would do what He would, and she'd be left to pick up the pieces.

Or maybe not.

Maybe this time, things would be different. Maybe she'd get the answer she sought. Maybe she'd find Sarah, healthy and whole. And maybe the faith Jasmine had searched so hard for would finally find her.

TWENTY

"Are you okay?" Eli moved up behind her, his arms sliding around her waist.

"No."

"We'll find her."

"You keep telling me that."

"I keep believing it."

"What did Jake say?" She turned in his arms, expecting him to loosen his hold, but he didn't, and the heat of his body warmed her, reminding her that no matter how bad things seemed, she wasn't alone.

"He's going to question McKenna, but he doesn't want to tip him off to the fact that we've spoken to Mary. He's afraid that…" His voice trailed off and he shook his head.

"What?"

"If McKenna did take Sarah, he did it because he wants to find Mary. Until he gets the information he wants from her, he'll keep her alive."

"But if he knows Mary has already told her story—"

"He'll have no reason to keep Sarah alive."

"I don't like this. I don't see how it can have a good ending."

"God can do anything, Jasmine. You know that."

"Sometimes I do."

"Jasmine?" Mary stepped outside, her blond hair pulled into a ponytail, her face pale.

"Yes?"

"I'm sorry I dragged Sarah into this. If I'd known…" She didn't finish the thought, but Jasmine knew the game she was playing with herself. If I'd known I would have, I could have, I might have. Jasmine had said the same things to herself hundreds of times in the past years.

"Don't blame yourself, Mary. You did what you thought was right." She meant it, but knew her words would be little comfort to the young woman.

"Maybe if I go back home and talk to the reverend, I can convince him to tell me where Sarah is."

"No way." Eli nearly barked the words, and Mary jumped.

"It was just a suggestion."

"If you go back home you'll be putting yourself in danger *and* you'll be giving McKenna a good reason to get rid of Sarah. What you need to do is stay here and keep doing what you've been doing while we try to figure out where McKenna could hide a grown woman."

"He lives alone. Maybe his house?" Jasmine doubted anyone would notice if Sarah were tied up in a room somewhere at the reverend's house.

"I don't think so." Mary moved back inside and grabbed a handbag from the counter. "He's got too many people in and out of there all the time. Plus a couple ladies from the church come in to clean for him twice a week. They volunteered when Rebecca started back to school."

"The church?" Jasmine knew she was grasping at straws, but suggested it anyway.

"Same problem. Too many people in and out. There's no way he could hide someone there." Mary led them around to the front of the house. "Look, I hate to cut and run, but I've got to be at work in a few minutes. If there's anything I can do to help, let me know."

"And if you think of anything that might help us find Sarah, let *us* know."

"All right. I'll be praying for Sarah. I hope you find her soon. I hope she's okay."

"Me, too." Jasmine watched as Mary drove away, her heart heavy in her chest.

"Don't look so sad, sugar. We've got a lot more information than we had when we got here."

"But we still don't have Sarah."

"We've got reason to believe she's alive. That counts for something."

"Maybe, but Mary has just confirmed what we suspected—McKenna is a killer. If he's got Sarah, there's no telling what he'll do to her."

"We've got time. As long as she doesn't tell him where Mary is, Sarah will be okay."

"I hope you're right, Eli."

"Of course, I'm right." He dropped an arm around her shoulders and he urged her forward along the dirt road, back toward his SUV.

By the time they made their way to the main road, the sun had risen in fingers of light that streaked across the sky and turned deep navy to cornflower-blue. Bare-branched trees stretched upward, gray skeletons reaching for what they'd never touch. It might have been a stark picture or a lonely one, but to Jasmine it was intensely beautiful, the colors seeping into the darkness like hope after despair, refreshing and breathtaking.

"It's beautiful, isn't it?" Eli spoke quietly, his Southern drawl slipping under the locked door of her heart, demanding attention.

"Yes."

"If Sarah can see it, she'll have a good reason to hope. Another day. Another chance that someone will find her."

"Do you always look on the bright side of things?"

"I look at both sides. Then I choose to focus my energy on the positive. Anything else is a waste of time."

"Maybe, but I like to be realistic."

"Realistic is good but sometimes it limits our possibilities. You're a good example of that. You had a dream. You pursued it. It didn't matter that the odds were against you. It didn't matter how unrealistic your goals were."

"You're talking about my writing career?"

"Sure. I've bought Jasmine Hart books for my nieces and nephews. Four Christmases ago your books were flying off the shelves faster than they could be restocked. Not many people have the confidence to go after a dream like that. They're caught up in the reality. They forget the possibilities."

It was true. She'd gone after her dream of writing and illustrating children's books with no thought to impossibilities. She'd known the market was tight. She'd known her chances were slim. Somehow, though, it hadn't mattered. She'd believed with everything she was that she'd succeed. Nothing, not rejection, not failure, not a million story ideas that didn't work, could convince her otherwise. "Things have changed. *I've* changed."

"Have you? Or have you just stopped letting yourself dream?"

"Dreams are for people who haven't lived a nightmare."

"Dreams are for anyone willing to believe in them." His words were gentle, his fingers warm as they slid along her arm and linked with hers.

"It isn't that easy."

"Nothing worthwhile is." He shot a smile in her direction,

then pulled the SUV into the parking lot of a pancake house. "Let's get something to eat and come up with our next plan of action."

"I'd rather head back to Sarah's. Jake might have found something out by now."

"Whether he has or not, there won't be much we can do to help with the investigation."

"I know, but—"

"Jasmine, the human body can't survive without fuel, and I'm about empty." He opened the door and stepped out into purplish dawn.

Jasmine hesitated, then did the same. "I'd really rather keep going."

"Sugar, you'd go until you couldn't go anymore. What good would that do Sarah?" He rounded the car and took her hand, his palm rough and calloused against her smooth skin. She wanted to hold on tight, believe that his optimism and faith would keep the worst from happening.

"Maybe you're right."

His cell phone rang and he answered it, his gaze steady on her as he spoke.

"Jennings. He wasn't? Yeah, it is strange. No. Nothing. Right. We'll be back as soon as we can." He shoved the phone in his pocket and turned toward the SUV. "I think we better get something on the road."

"What's going on?"

"That was Jake. He went to visit the reverend, but McKenna was out."

"At six in the morning?"

"That's not all. He decided to visit with Mary's parents, as well. The mother was home, but Jackson was out."

"Did Laura say where her husband was?"

"Out visiting a parishioner who'd suddenly taken ill and

been transported to the hospital. The only problem is when Jake sent a man to the hospital, Jackson wasn't there."

"They're together."

"That's what Jake thinks. That, and that they're with Sarah."

"Where?"

"That's the question of the hour." Eli grimaced and pulled open the door for Jasmine. Much as he wanted to stay positive about the outcome, he couldn't help worrying. Sarah's health was fragile. Desperate men wouldn't care about that.

"You're worried." Jasmine spoke as he started the engine, her gaze filled with anxiety. She looked pale, fatigue etching fine lines near the corners of her mouth.

"I didn't expect both men to be part of this. I thought one or the other had taken her."

"And the fact that they both have her makes the situation worse?"

"I don't know, but I don't like it."

"You're not the only one. Jackson was angry enough to do something desperate. With or without information about his daughter, he may harm Sarah." Jasmine's fear vibrated through her words, and Eli wanted to pull the SUV over, take her into his arms and convince her that everything was going to be okay.

He settled for sliding his hand under the heavy fall of her hair, kneading the tense muscles in her neck. Her skin was cool and smooth. Her hair as soft as spun silk. Her lips had been, too, but now wasn't the time to be thinking about that. "We don't know anything for sure, so let's not speculate."

"Then what should we do?"

"Keep driving and keep praying. Eventually we'll be at the end of the road and know where we've been heading."

"And have Sarah safely home?"

"Yes." He agreed because she needed him to, and because

he had to believe that God wouldn't take Jasmine's mother-in-law. Jasmine had already lost too much for one lifetime.

His stomach growled, but he ignored it. Military life had taught him to tough things out, to stick to the goal and to not let anything, even his own weaknesses, keep him from achieving the objective. Right now the objective was to get back to Lakeview, talk to Jake, then go hunting for Reverend McKenna and Jackson. They couldn't stay away for long before they were missed. They knew that, and unless Eli missed his guess, they'd be home long before they thought that would happen. Unfortunately for them, they'd already been missed and they'd have a lot of explaining to do when they returned home. Whether or not Jake could get either of them to admit anything remained to be seen.

The SUV bounced over a rut in the road, jarring Eli's already throbbing leg. Most days the injuries he'd received didn't bother him much, but he'd been in the car too long and he was definitely suffering for it. He needed some Tylenol, a long walk and a heating pad, in that order. First, though, he needed to find Sarah. He'd told Jasmine that her mother-in-law would be okay. He'd do whatever it took to make sure that was true. God willing, that would be enough.

TWENTY-ONE

By the time Eli pulled up in front of Sarah's small rancher, the sun was high in the sky, its watery light only partially warming the frigid air.

"Finally." Jasmine barely waited for the car to stop before she opened the door and hopped out, then raced up the porch steps and into the house.

Eli followed more slowly, letting the knotted muscles in his leg ease before he attempted the stairs. The last thing he needed after the long night was to wind up on his backside in the cold grass.

Jasmine reappeared in the doorway as he stepped onto the porch. "She's still not here."

"You were hoping she would be?"

"I don't know. Maybe." She smiled, the expression sad enough to make Eli's heart ache.

"Give it another few hours and she'll be sitting in the easy chair reading one of those romance novels I've seen lying around the house."

"A few hours is an eternity when someone you love is missing. I'm going to call Jake and see if he's tracked down Jackson or McKenna." She stepped aside as Eli moved into the house, the subtle sweet scent of her hovering in the air, clinging to Eli as if it were part of him.

"He said he'd call as soon as he knew something." Not that Eli planned to wait around to hear from him. As soon as he got Jasmine settled in, he was heading out to Fellowship Community Church.

"Maybe he got caught up in something and forgot."

"I don't think Lakeview is crime ridden enough for Jake to forget a missing woman." He placed a hand over Jasmine's before she could lift the phone. "Sometimes the best thing we can do is give the experts time to do their jobs."

"You're suggesting I just wait around for Jake to call?"

"That's exactly what I'm suggesting."

"Forget it." She lifted the phone, dialed the number, her eyes blazing into his. After a moment, she scowled, left a brief message on Jake's voice mail and hung up. "He didn't pick up."

"Maybe he's interviewing one of his suspects."

"Maybe. I just wish I *knew* something." She yawned, settling down onto the sofa, her curly hair falling across her cheeks as she rested her head in her hands.

"It's been a long twenty-four hours, Jasmine. I think we both need to get some rest. We'll be able to tackle the problem more efficiently if we aren't sleep deprived."

"I don't think I can sleep. Not until Sarah is home."

"Just close your eyes for a few minutes." He patted one of the pillows on the couch, and Jasmine smiled wearily.

"Do you ever give up, Eli?"

"Not when I really want something."

"And you really want me to rest?"

"Among other things."

Her pale cheeks reddened at his words, and she grabbed the pillow, kicked off her shoes and lay down on her side. Obviously, she'd rather sleep than contemplate what he'd meant by his comment. That was fine by Eli.

He grabbed a colorful blanket that was hanging over the easy chair and covered Jasmine with it. Her eyes were already closing, the dark crescents beneath them like bruises against her pallid skin.

He brushed silky strands of hair from her cheek, let his fingers linger against her warm skin for just a moment.

"If you're okay here by yourself, I'm going to go back up to my cabin." For a quick shower and some Tylenol. Then he was going out, but he didn't think Jasmine needed to know that, so he left out the details of his plan.

"I've been okay by myself for years, Eli. A few hours isn't going to hurt me."

He knew she hadn't meant the words to be sad, but they were, and he leaned down to brush a kiss against her forehead. "Call my cell phone if you need me."

"Call mine if *you* need *me*." She grinned and Eli knew he could stay where he was for the rest of the day, watching Jasmine rest, making sure she was okay.

That wouldn't get him any closer to his objective, though, so he said goodbye, stepping out into the chilly afternoon, his mind racing ahead. Time was running out for Sarah. He needed to find her now. As he climbed into his SUV and drove up the hill to the cabin, he prayed that it wasn't already too late.

Jasmine was dreaming.

She and John on the dock, holding hands, staring out over the lake as they had so many times. She could smell his aftershave, the spicy, fragrant stuff he loved so much, could feel the smoothness of his palm, the heat of his arm pressed against hers. She looked up into his eyes, saw that he was watching her, a half smile on his face. "What will you do when I'm gone?"

"Miss you."

"Not forever."

"For as long as it takes for you to come home."

"People can't always come home."

"Of course they can. If they want to badly enough."

"Look." He pointed out into the lake, and Jasmine saw a canoe moving toward them. "That's my ride."

"You don't have to go."

"Sure I do. The girls are waiting for me."

"Then I'll come with you."

"Maybe later. Right now, we don't have a big enough boat."

He was right. The closer the canoe got, the easier it was to see how small it was. How completely inadequate for carrying two adults. Her heart ached with the knowledge, her stomach churning with the sick, sad feeling of loss. "I don't want you to go."

"I have to, but it's not forever. We'll see each other again."

"I don't want to be left behind." The words were a sob of anguish that spilled from the very depth of her soul.

"You're not being left behind. You're being given more time to get ready for the trip. There's a difference." He smiled the same sweet smile she'd loved from the first moment she'd seen it, then kissed her with passion, with love.

Suddenly Jasmine was alone on the dock, the boat hundreds of yards out, moving away with alarming speed. She jumped into the water, ready to swim after it, but someone grabbed her arm, dragging her back onto the dock.

"You need to stop asking why they died and start asking why you lived," Eli whispered in her ear, his lips warm against her skin, and she turned to look into his eyes, saw something there she never thought she'd see again—a future filled with promise.

* * *

A phone rang, yanking Jasmine from the dream, and she jumped up, her heart pounding, her head still muzzy from sleep.

"Hello?"

"Jasmine?" The feminine voice was familiar, but Jasmine couldn't quite place it.

"Yes."

"This is Mary."

At the name, Jasmine's thoughts were suddenly sharp and sure. "Are you okay?"

"Fine. It's just… Well, this might be stupid, but I was thinking about what we were talking about. You know, where the reverend could hide a grown woman and I was thinking maybe there was a place."

"Where?" Jasmine grabbed paper and pencil, her hands shaking so hard she wasn't sure she'd be able to write.

"The church owns a camp. The youth group goes there at least once every summer. A couple of acres in the mountains with cabins and stuff. It's probably nothing, but I just can't get it out of my head."

"Do you have an address?"

"No, but it's easy to find. Go up past the church. Maybe fifteen miles. There's a dirt road off to the right with a sign that says Fellowship Campground. It can be kind of hard to see in the summer, but I think in the winter you'll be able to find it no problem."

"Thanks, Mary."

"You'll call me when you find her?"

"Of course." Jasmine hung up the phone, all the fog gone from her brain. She needed to call Jake and Eli, get them both up to the campground.

She dialed Jake's number, tamping down frustration when

his voice mail picked up. The message she left was brief and to the point. She was going to Fellowship Campground and she hoped he'd meet her there.

Next, she tried the cabin, letting the phone ring until the answering machine picked up. She left the same message for Eli that she'd left for Jake, repeating the same on his cell-phone voice mail.

That was it, then. She was on her own.

She grabbed her purse and keys, considered taking a knife or some other weapon, then thought better of it. She'd go into the camp quietly and pray she saw danger before it saw her. The other option was waiting for Jake or Eli to return her call. There was no way she planned to do that. Not with Sarah in danger.

Minutes later, she was in Sarah's beat-up old Chevy, driving toward Peaks of Otter, her mouth dry with fear and anxiety, her hands tight around the steering wheel.

"Please, Lord, let her be there. Please. Let her be all right." The prayer was a litany that she whispered over and over again as she wound her way into the mountains, past Fellowship Community Church, then farther up the narrowing paved road. The trees closed in around her, their branches scraping the roof of the car as she drove. Despite bright sunlight, the road seemed dark and shadowy, the deep woods on either side filled with danger. She could imagine eyes staring out at her from the thick foliage, imagine that the bare branches were arms reaching out to stop her.

"Cut it out. You're scaring yourself silly over nothing." She hissed the words out loud, but they did little to quiet the frantic pounding of her heart. There was danger here. Whether real or imagined she didn't know. All she was sure of was that she was going to Fellowship Campground and she was going to check every cabin. If Sarah was in one of them, she'd find her.

She was just beginning to wonder if Mary's directions had been wrong when she spotted the sign. Old and worn, the painted wood had faded so that the words were barely legible. She slowed the car, squinted to read what must have once been bright blue but now looked gray. Fellowship Campground.

Finally.

She turned onto the gravel road, then remembered Eli's warning earlier that morning when they'd been approaching Mary's house. If Jackson or McKenna was at the camp, she didn't want to let them know she was coming. With that in mind, she U-turned, scraping the sides of Sarah's car on thick pine branches. She drove a half mile away from the sign before she was able to pull the car off the road and park it.

Now back to the faded sign, the gravel road, the camp. Cold air slapped at her cheeks as she jogged the way she'd come, her ears straining for any hint that other people were around. She heard nothing but her own gasping breath and the soft rustle of leaves beneath her feet. The gravel road twisted through thick forest, leading upward at an incline that left Jasmine breathless.

She rounded a curve and nearly walked into a large black sedan. Her heart skipped a beat, and she scrambled for cover, ducking behind a tree, peeking out from behind it. There was no one in the car. Nothing moving near it. A few cabins dotted the area. Boarded up and lonely looking. Was Sarah in one of them? Was McKenna with her? Someone had to have driven the car, and Jasmine knew for sure it hadn't been her mother-in-law.

She crept forward, her heart slamming in her chest, her body cold with fear. One cautious step at a time, she moved toward the closest cabin, eased around to its door, reached for the doorknob. Should she open it? Knock? Announce her presence? Try to keep it hidden? Did it matter?

Before she could make a decision, a soft noise drifted on the cold afternoon air. A click that barely carried to her ears, but made the hair on the back of her neck stand on end. She knew that sound. Had heard it in movies and on television, and she knew it never meant anything good. A gun being cocked, a killer getting ready.

She expected to feel a bullet slam into her back, but nothing happened and she turned slowly, looking for the gunman.

Tall, gaunt, long hair falling loose around his shoulders, Reverend McKenna stood in the doorway of the cabin across the campground from Jasmine. He looked a decade older, his face pale and long, his skin yellowish, his eyes burning like hot coals as he pointed a rifle at her heart. "I thought I heard a car. Sarah will be happy to have a visitor."

At the mention of her mother-in-law's name, Jasmine forgot about the gun and her fear and moved toward the man. "Where is she?"

"Inside. I've provided comfortable accommodations for her. Not that she deserves it after what she's done to my congregation."

"You're the one who's destroyed your church, Reverend. Not Sarah."

"I'd watch your tone, young lady. I don't find mouthy women attractive." He frowned, motioning her forward with the tip of the rifle. "May as well come in. And don't try anything funny. You go running off and I'll kill Sarah and then come looking for you."

"You're sick."

"I'm smart. I know what's right and what's wrong and when I see something that's wrong, I fix it."

"Like you fixed Rebecca."

"Exactly like that. Now come on. Maybe having you here

will convince Sarah to give me what I want." He grabbed her arm, dragged her into the dimly lit cabin and shoved her with enough strength to send her sprawling.

She landed hard, the breath leaving her lungs, stars shooting through her head.

"Jazz?" Sarah's voice was weak, raspy, but so welcome Jasmine almost cried.

"You're alive!" She scrambled to her feet, raced toward the chair where Sarah was sitting. No. Not sitting. Tied. Arms and legs bound to hard wood.

"She won't be for long if one of you doesn't tell me what I want to know. Where's Mary?" McKenna growled the words, crossing the room in two long strides, dragging Jasmine to her feet and pressing the barrel of the rifle under her chin. "Did you hear the question, old lady? Where is Mary? Tell me or your daughter-in-law gets it."

Sarah met Jasmine's gaze, regret and fear coloring her eyes deep-navy. "I don't know."

"You're a meddling old witch and you know exactly where she is. So tell me now." He jabbed the barrel of the rifle hard against Jasmine's flesh, knocking her teeth together. Then swung it downward, slamming it so hard into her side, she gasped, pain shooting through her ribs.

"Okay. Okay. I'll tell you." Sarah spoke quickly, and Jasmine shook her head.

"Don't tell him anything, Sarah. The sheriff and Eli are on their way here. He's out of time."

"You're lying." McKenna slammed the gun into her ribs again, and Jasmine wondered if her time on earth was up. Wasted time. Time that could have been spent pursuing life rather than mourning the dead. *I am so sorry, Lord. So sorry I didn't take what you gave me.*

Now it was too late.

Don't give up. Distract him. Get the gun.

The words danced through her mind like a butterfly's kiss, like a little girl's laughter, like hope renewed.

She twisted in McKenna's arms, trying to move a fraction of an inch away from the rifle barrel, knowing she was going to have to fight. For Sarah. For herself. For another chance. "I'm not lying. Listen. I think I hear a car."

"Liar. You know what the Bible says about liars? They should be punished. By death."

Jasmine grabbed the barrel of the rifle, shoving it backward as he pulled the trigger.

The sound of a gunshot ripped through the silence of the mountain, and Eli lunged forward racing up the gravel path that led to the campground, Jake close on his heels. Several other officers were running, too, fanning out, surrounding the clearing and the six cabins there.

Another shot followed the first. Then a scream. A thud. A curse.

"The middle cabin on the left. Go, go, go. Eli, stay back. You're not armed." Jake was shouting the words, but they barely registered as Eli slammed his shoulder into the cabin door, felt the wood splinter and crack.

He backed up, kicked hard, slammed his shoulder into the wood again, nearly falling into the cabin as the door gave completely.

"Freeze! Police!" Jake shouted the command, shoving past Eli, trying to force him out of the line of fire.

Eli rolled with it, coming to his feet in one smooth move that brought him into the center of the cabin, seeing it all in a glance. Jasmine on the floor, bleeding. Sarah tied up in a chair. McKenna with the rifle pointed toward the door. Then pointed toward himself, pushing it up under his chin.

"No way you're going to get off so easily." He leaped

forward, yanking the gun out of McKenna's hand, swinging it around and knocking him hard on the temple with the butt.

"Hey, cool it, man." Jake grabbed the rifle, and Eli let it go, dropping onto the ground next to Jasmine. Blood spilled out from under her, a dark wet pool of it that reminded him of that long-ago day when he'd lost so many friends. He wouldn't lose Jasmine. He couldn't lose her.

"Sugar, you with me?" He pressed his finger to her neck, felt the steady pulse of her heart and nearly sagged with relief as her eyes opened.

"I thought you'd never get here."

"Where are you hurt?"

"Everywhere. But mostly my arm. I don't think it's serious. The bullet just kind of grazed me." She smiled wanly, struggling to sit up.

He gently pushed her back down, stripping off his jacket, pressing it against the deep gash visible in her upper arm. "Don't move. Jake, we need an ambulance for Jasmine and for Sarah."

"I'm already on it." The sheriff had handed McKenna off to another officer and was untying Sarah, speaking quietly to her as he removed the ropes from her arm.

"Sarah?" Jasmine pushed against Eli's hold, levering up so she could see her mother-in-law. "Are you okay?"

"Am *I* okay? I'm not the one lying bleeding on the floor."

"I'm not bleeding. Much." She glanced down at the blood, blanched and swayed.

"Lie back. You're losing a lot of blood." Eli's heart was racing a mile a minute, his hands unsteady as he tried to maintain pressure on the wound. What if an artery had been nicked? What if she bled to death before the ambulance arrived? What if…

"Hey." Jasmine pressed a hand to his cheek, her palm warm and soft. "I'm okay. Really."

"Yeah, well, you almost weren't, and I'm not quite over that yet. I just found you. I'm not ready to lose you." He lifted her hand, pressed a kiss to her palm.

"That's good, because I'm not ready to be lost."

Her words gave him pause, and he met her gaze, saw something there he hadn't expected—peace. "I think we have a lot to talk about after you heal."

"Maybe even before then." She smiled, swayed again.

"Okay. That's it. Down you go." He eased her back down, worry thrumming at his nerves again.

"Sorry, I'm just a little woozy."

"You're going to be fine." *Please, God, let her be fine.*

Sirens screamed their warning, and Eli started to rise, wanting to go out to the road, make sure the ambulance didn't miss the sign, pass the camp and waste precious time.

Jasmine's hand closed over his, pulling him back. "Don't leave me."

He looked down into her eyes, blue-green and blazing with emotions, and settled back down beside her. "Not even if you begged me to go."

TWENTY-TWO

The first five stitches hurt. By the time the E.R. doctor put in the final fifteen, Jasmine could barely feel them. Barely.

"That's it. You're all set." The doctor wrapped the wound, handed her home-care instructions. "I'm prescribing painkillers for the cracked ribs. No heavy lifting, nothing that could cause further injury. You need to rest and heal. Make an appointment with your primary doctor for a follow-up visit. You'll need the stitches out in ten days."

"All right."

"You've got someone to drive you home?"

"I—" Thought she had, but Eli hadn't appeared, and she was wondering if he'd come to the hospital at all. "I'll find someone. Right now, I need to see my mother-in-law, Sarah Hart. She was brought in at the same time as me."

"We'll be keeping her overnight. She's dehydrated and has a concussion. Someone gave her quite a knock on the head. She's in room 301. How about I have the nurse bring you up to her room?"

"I'm sure I can find it."

"I'm sure you can, too, but you lost a lot of blood and I don't want you passing out on the way there. If you haven't found a ride by the time you want to leave, we'll call you a cab. Stay here. The nurse will be in shortly."

Shortly turned into five minutes. Then ten. Fifteen minutes after the doctor had walked out, Jasmine was still waiting. "And I'm not waiting anymore."

She stood, swayed, got her balance. "Okay. I'm fine. A little walk through the hospital isn't beyond me. After all, it was just a flesh wound."

"Talking to yourself?" Eli's warm drawl washed over her, and she whirled toward him, blackness edging her vision at the too-quick movement.

"Whoa. Slow down, sugar." He scooped her into his arms, the movement so fluid and effortless Jasmine didn't have time to protest.

"I'm okay, but you won't be if you keep carrying me. You've got a bad leg."

"And it doesn't hurt a bit when I'm with you." He grinned, that boy-next-door smile that made her heart melt. She'd never thought another man would touch her the way John had, but Eli had done it, slipping past her guard and settling in.

He carried her to the hall, lowered her into a wheelchair that sat near the nurses station. "I don't think they'll mind if we borrow this for a while. Where are we headed?"

"Room 301."

"To see Sarah?"

"Yes, they had to admit her. The doctor said it's only for observation. She should be fine."

"I'm glad. When I heard the gunshot, I thought I'd lost you both."

"McKenna was crazy enough to kill us. It's only by the grace of God he didn't."

"Not for lack of effort. He's been charged with attempted murder. There may be more charges once Jake finishes his investigation." Eli's gruff tone couldn't hide the pain in his voice, and Jasmine turned to look up into his face.

"What aren't you telling me?"

"They found Rebecca. That's why I wasn't here sooner. I needed to call Marcus and tell him that his sister will never be coming home."

"McKenna really did kill her." She felt sick with the knowledge, horrified by the reverend's disregard for life.

"One of Jake's men found her remains in an old storage shed at the camp. It looks like she was killed by blunt-force trauma to the head, but we won't know for sure until the coroner finishes his investigation."

"I'm so sorry."

"Me, too. Marcus is pretty torn up. He's got emergency leave and he'll be coming home to bury her." He shook his head. "Jake is going to try and get the body of McKenna's first wife exhumed. He wants to have it tested for poison."

"The reverend was a sick man."

"Or an evil one. I can't decide which. All I know is that at least one woman is dead because of him and a family has been torn apart."

"What do you mean?"

"Jackson Cornell has made a full confession to his part in things. He'd heard from a friend of Mary's—"

"Niki?" Jasmine remembered the young pregnant woman at the potluck.

"I think that was the name. She told Cornell that Sarah might have helped Mary leave town. He confronted Sarah at the grand opening of the museum. She denied knowing anything, but he didn't believe her. He saw an opportunity to get back at her, and shoved her down the stairs. He figured he could get her out of the way, search her house, find information about his daughter."

"It didn't work out that way."

"No. She lived, and he felt guiltier than he expected. He went to McKenna who assured him he'd acted righteously. They've been working together since then, trying to find Mary. According to Jackson, he had no idea the reverend had murdered Rebecca. All he knew was that he wanted to find his daughter and that Reverend McKenna was anxious to help. When they learned that both you and Sarah were out of the house Wednesday night, McKenna drove over, planning to break in and search for information."

"But Sarah was there."

"Yeah. McKenna knocked on the door, Sarah opened it, invited him in."

"And he knocked her out and took her to the cabin."

"That's what Jackson is saying."

"Does Jake believe him?"

"Yeah, but being innocent of murder doesn't make him less guilty of assault. He's going to jail for a long time."

"Poor Laura."

"She's lost her husband, but she's got her daughter back."

"I'm not sure if she'll be happy with the trade."

"It's better than the alternative—Mary dead. Probably Jackson dead, too. There's no way McKenna would have let him live."

"You're right." He hadn't even spared his own wife. Poor Rebecca, everything she'd wanted, everything she'd dreamed, cut short by a man who had no love for anyone or anything. Her own husband. "Rebecca didn't even have a chance. How could she ever be prepared to defend herself against a man she loved?"

"She couldn't. That's probably why McKenna succeeded in his attack."

"She was way too young to die. Especially in such a

horrible way. What a waste of a life." Jasmine shuddered, and Eli stopped pushing the wheelchair, came around in front of her, crouching so they were eye to eye.

"We might mourn for a life cut short, but a life lived for God is never wasted. No matter how few years there are, they will always be enough."

"I never thought of it that way."

"Most people don't. They only see that a life is cut short. They never think it was exactly the amount of time it was meant to be. Come on. This is Sarah's room. We'll visit for a few minutes, then I'm taking you home and getting you settled in before I go pick Gran up. Her plane is coming in at seven. It won't do for me to be late."

"Your grandmother is coming?"

"Sure is. I didn't want you staying in the house alone tonight, and I didn't think it would be appropriate for me to stay with you."

"I'm sure Germaine would have been happy to help."

"Sure she would have, but she would have talked your ear off all night. You need your rest. Besides, Gran has been dying to meet you. This gives her the perfect excuse."

"You told her about me?"

"She likes to know about the important people in my life."

"Eli—"

"You *are* important to me, Jasmine. And every day I know you, you're more important."

"You always have the perfect words to say."

"It's only the truth." He ran a finger over her lips, his eyes darkening. "But I don't want to scare you. You may run to New Hampshire and make me chase you into even colder territory. You know how much I despise the cold."

Jasmine smiled, grabbing his hand, pressing it to her cheek. "I'm not scared. Maybe a little sad, but not scared."

"Sad, scared, worried. Whatever you feel, I'll be here for you. Forever."

"Forever isn't ever long enough."

"Forever is whatever we make of it." He placed a soft kiss on her lips, smoothed the hair back from her face, stared into her eyes. "Ready?"

"Ready."

For today. For tomorrow. For whatever would come. For living life instead of mourning death. For accepting what couldn't be changed. For embracing her own fragile faith, building it up, allowing herself to dream again. Whatever God had for her. Whatever He planned. She *was* ready.

EPILOGUE

Warm rain fell from the steel-gray sky, splashing into Smith Mountain Lake and washing the landscape in dazzling color. Bright greens, deep yellows, dark purples. The area around Sarah's rancher bloomed with new life. Spring had finally come.

Jasmine stepped around the side of the house, her heart hammering a slow, hard beat as rain drenched the baseball hat she wore and slid into her eyes. It was time. She'd known it was coming, but now, with her wedding less than a week away, she couldn't put it off any longer.

The azaleas were bright pink and vibrant against the rancher's white siding. There, beneath their sheltering blossoms, dark gray wood sparkled with moisture. Jasmine picked it up, tracing the weather-smoothed letters, her mind racing back in time. John. Maddie. Megan. Her heart ached with love for them, with the desire to see their faces, hear their laughter, feel their arms wrap around her once again.

"Death is goodbye for just a little while. One day we'll meet again. For now, I'll hold you in my heart and in my memories." Tears mixed with the rain that slid down her cheeks, but she didn't wipe them away. Grief would always be there just below the surface, but she wouldn't let it define who she was. She'd grown stronger, more sure, more able to understand her place in the world. Her purpose. God had one for her, of that she was sure, the faith she'd never quite been able to grasp growing like a tiny seed that had only been waiting for sunlight before it bloomed.

She walked toward the lake, wet grass slick under her feet, the wood cool in her hands, the scent of new life in the air. Grass, rain, flowers dancing on the breeze that blew in over the lake. She stepped onto the dock and sat down with her feet hanging over the edge, her fingers tracing the letters one last time. John. Maddie. Megan.

A soft sound mixed with the splash of rain. Footsteps on wood. Warm hands cupped her shoulders, kneaded her neck, and then Eli was beside her, sitting on the dock, pressed close to her side, his hazel eyes staring into hers as if he could see everything she felt.

"I thought I saw you come this way."

"And you followed me?"

"I love you too much not to."

"I love you, too." She glanced down at the wood, smiling through her tears. "That's why it's time to say goodbye."

He didn't ask what she meant. He knew. She saw it in his eyes, felt it in the gentle caress of his fingers on her arm. "Do you want me to leave or stay?"

"Stay." She lifted the wood, tears coming faster and harder until she was shaking with them. "I couldn't say goodbye at the funeral. It was just too hard."

"You don't have to say it now, sugar. They're your family. For always. Nothing we have together will ever change that." Eli wrapped her in his arms, sandwiching the wood between them, completing the circle of connection that brought her new life and old life together. Love.

She sniffed back her tears, pulling back and looking up into Eli's eyes. "Goodbye shouldn't hurt so much."

"Goodbye always hurts, but it's never forever."

"No. Not forever. Goodbye, my darlings." She pressed a kiss to her fingers and touched each name once, then let the wood drop, watching as it drifted out into the lake and slowly disappeared.

Warm rain. Hot tears. An end. A beginning. All part of the life God had planned for her.

"Are you okay?" Eli's broad palms slid down her cheeks, wiping away the moisture, easing some of the pain.

"How could I not be when you're here with me?" She wrapped her arms around his waist and let him hold her there in the rain with the scent of flowers and earth and hope dancing around them.

* * * * *

Be sure to pick up Shirlee McCoy's next book.
THE GUARDIAN'S MISSION,
coming in August 2008,
only from Love Inspired Suspense.

Dear Reader,

God never promised that life would be easy for us just because we trust in Him. He only promised that He'll be with us through everything. When the unimaginable happens, our belief in that promise may be shaken, but God's faithfulness remains true.

This is a lesson Jasmine Hart learns after she loses her husband and daughters in a tragic accident. When her mother-in-law needs help after surgery, Jasmine returns to the place where memories are around every corner and where peaceful dreams are hard to come by. Though her greatest desire is to avoid reminders of what she's lost, she learns that only in embracing the past and all its heartaches can she move into the future.

I hope you enjoy reading Jasmine's story, and I pray that whatever you face in life, you'll know the truth of God's love and faithfulness.

Blessings,

Shirlee McCoy

QUESTIONS FOR DISCUSSION

1. For years Jasmine had it all. When everything she loves most is taken from her, she feels as if her life is over. How does that attitude affect her relationship with Sarah? How does it affect her relationship with God?

2. Returning to Lakeview is a necessity that Jasmine wishes she could avoid. Still, she agrees to help Sarah. What is her motivation for doing so?

3. When Jasmine returned to Lakeview, she finds that things have changed more than she'd imagined they would. How does this make her feel?

4. Her mother-in-law's financial difficulties only add to Jasmine's guilt. Why does Jasmine choose to pay the bills rather than confront Sarah with what she's learned?

5. Jasmine seems more comfortable avoiding relationships than being in them. Despite those feelings, she finds herself attracted to Eli. What is her response to that?

6. Eli comes to Lakeview to search for a friend's missing sister. Have you ever done something for a dear friend, even though it was difficult? What was it?

7. What qualities attract Jasmine to Eli? How does she view him in light of the relationship she had with her husband?

8. Eli mentions he grew up in a household full of women, including his mother, sisters and grandmother. Do you think this makes him more or less attractive? Why or why not?

9. Jasmine has difficulty forgiving herself for what happens to her husband and daughters. How is false guilt destroying her life? Have you ever experienced such guilt about things you have no control over? How did you deal with it?

10. It is easy to dwell on our sorrows and disappointments. Is that what Jasmine does?

11. How might having a stronger belief in God's mercy and love have comforted her during her grief?

12. As Christians we understand that there is life after death. That doesn't make saying goodbye to those we love any easier. How does Jasmine finally say goodbye to her family?

13. God brings Eli into Jasmine's life at just the right time. Have there been times in your life when God has given you a special friend to help you through difficulties?